A Goode Girls Romance

Courting Trouble

KERRIGAN BYRNE

OLIVER
HEBER
BOOKS

To my Anam Cara.
I recognized you instantly and never looked back.

PROLOGUE

CHARITON'S DOCK, SOUTHWARK,
LONDON, 1880

*A*s Honoria's blood pooled onto the dock from the bullet wound, she felt oddly relieved.

She was ready to die.

Marriage to William Mosby, the Viscount Woodhaven, had first stripped her of any innocence she'd had left. Then of her joy. Her confidence. And finally, her decency.

To slake her unceasing misery—or perhaps in defiance of her tyrant of a husband—she'd taken a handful of lovers over the years. One of those lovers, George Hamby-Forsyth, the Earl of Sutherland, had offered to marry her younger sister Prudence when Honoria had ended their affair.

William had forbidden Nora to tell Prudence about her previous affair. He'd threatened to ruin her sister and to visit tortures upon her she hadn't yet conceived of.

So she'd obeyed him.

She obeyed him!

How could she have been so stupid? So utterly selfish and blind? Her life was *already* a torment, and the ultimate torture was a marriage to the wrong man.

If Nora knew anything, it was that.

1

William had used her father's shipping company to smuggle cocaine into the country. He had sought out her lovers and murdered them, framing Prudence for the deed.

Her sister might have hanged if not for the protection of her new husband, Chief Inspector Carlton Morley.

As Morley closed in on him, William had baited Prudence to use as a hostage to escape the city. But first, he'd stopped at her father's Southwark warehouse to tear through stacks of crates, apparently searching for one full of money he'd had delivered.

Nora stood helpless as William held a gun to her precious younger sister's head.

Morley perched above on the warehouse roof, aiming his rifle at William, his shot frustrated as the bastard used Pru as a human shield.

All this could have been avoided if she'd not been a selfish coward.

Honoria often read that people heard a rushing in their ears or felt their hearts pounding against their rib cages before they did something reckless or heroic.

But facing the consequences of her actions, of her husband's treachery, tore her heart out of her chest. So, it didn't beat faster. Her blood didn't rush around.

She felt—numb. Detached. As if she no longer inhabited her body.

As if she'd died long ago.

And maybe she had.

Taking a breath, Honoria had stepped into the doorway and faced the man she hated most in this world. She'd taken in his thinning ashen hair, yellowed teeth, and expanding paunch, the consequence of a life devoted to vice and villainy. It was as if his viciousness and malevolence was beginning to seep from the insides and corrupt his physical body.

He'd taken the gun from her sister's temple, and shot her, instead.

As she fell, she watched Morley avenge his wife, putting William down for good with one shot from his powerful rifle.

Somehow, Nora had made it outside...and was looking up at the sky when she heard Prudence scream her name. Then her dear sister's face was hovering above her, dark eyes wild with fear.

With her last breaths, Nora tried to make things right. "I'm sorry. I should have told you...I...was afraid..."

"Shh. Shh. Shh," Prudence soothed. "I didn't know what he was. What he was doing to you. No wonder you strayed. I'm not angry about George. Please don't blame yourself. Just—"

"I love you." Nora forced the words through the burning pain. "We don't say any of that, do we? We Goodes. But I do. I love you."

"I love you too," Pru sobbed, tears leaking from the tip of her nose. "I will for a long time, so don't start saying that like you mean goodbye."

"You are a wonderful sister. And I...I'm not..."

She began to fade then, unable to feel the warmth of the afternoon sun, even though it still alighted on her face.

And then she heard *his* name.

Titus Conleith.

It brought her back to life, if only for a moment. She clawed at Prudence, begging for him. Pleading. Knowing it was too late.

Yes, she deserved to die, and worse.

Because long ago, she'd broken a boy. A beautiful boy with a true heart and a pure soul.

That sin had been unforgivable.

And she'd spent the last decade paying the price.

THE COAL BOY

LONDON, NOVEMBER 1865

*T*itus Conleith had often fantasized about seeing Honoria Goode naked.

He'd been in an excruciating kind of love with her since he was a lad of ten. Now that he was undoubtedly a *man* at fourteen, his love had shifted.

Matured, he dared wager.

What he felt for her was a soft sort of reverence, a kind of awestruck incredulity at the sight of her each day. It was simply hard to believe a creature like her existed. That she moved about on this earth. In the house in which he *lived*.

That she was three years his senior at seventeen years of age was irrelevant, as was the fact that she stood three inches above him, more in her lace boots with the delicate heels. It mattered not that there existed no reality in which he could even approach her. That he could dare address her.

The idea of being with her in any capacity was so far beyond comprehension, it didn't bear consideration. He was the household boy-of-all-work for her father, Clarence Goode, the Baron of Cresthaven. Lower, even, than the chambermaid. He swept chimneys and fetched things, mucked stables and cleaned up after dogs that ate better than he did.

When he and Honoria shared a room, he was beneath her feet, sometimes quite literally.

One of his favorite memories was perhaps a year prior when she'd scheduled to ride her horse in the country paddock and no mounting block could be found. Titus had been called to lace his hands together so Honoria might use them as a step up into her saddle.

He'd seen the top of her boot that day, and a flash of the lily-white stocking over her calf as he'd presumed to help slide her foot into the stirrup.

It was the first time she'd truly looked at him. The first time their eyes locked, as the sun had haloed around her midnight curls like one of those chipped, expensive paintings of the Madonna that hung in the Baron's gallery.

In that moment, her features had been just as full of grace.

"You're bleeding," she'd remarked, flicking her gaze to a shallow wound on the flesh of his palm where a splinter on a shovel handle had gouged deep enough to draw blood. Her boot had ground a bit of dirt into the wound.

And he'd barely felt the pain.

Titus had balled his fist and hid it behind his back, lowering his gaze. "Inn't nothing, miss."

Reaching into her pocket, she'd drawn out a pressed white handkerchief and dangled it in front of him. "I didn't see it, or I'd not have—"

"Honoria!" her mother had reprimanded, eyeing him reprovingly as she trotted her own mare between them, obliging him to leap back lest he be trampled. "To dawdle with them is an unkindness, as you oblige them to inter-action they are not trained for. Really, you know better."

Honoria hadn't said a word, nor did she look back as she'd obediently cantered away at her mother's side.

But he'd retrieved her handkerchief from where it'd floated to the ground in her wake.

From that day on, it was her image painted on the backs of his eyelids when he closed them at night. Even when the scent of rose water had faded from his treasure.

Today, two of the three maids in the household had been too ill to work, and so the harried housekeeper tasked Titus with hauling the kindling into the east wing of the Mayfair manse to lay and light the fires before the family roused.

He'd done the master's first, then the mistress's, and had skipped Honoria's room for the nursery where the seven-year-old twins, Mercy and Felicity, slept.

Felicity had been huddled in bed, her golden head bent over a book as she squinted in the early morning gloom. The sweet-natured girl had given him a shy little wave as he tiptoed in and lit her a warm fire.

Against the mores of propriety, she'd thanked him in a whisper, and blushed when he'd given her a two-fingered salute before shutting the door behind him with a barely audible click. After tending to the hearths of the governess and the second-eldest Goode sister, Prudence, Titus finally found himself at Honoria's door.

He peered about the hall guiltily before admonishing himself for being ridiculous.

He was supposed to be here. It wouldn't do to squander this stroke of luck and not take any opportunity he could to be near her.

Alone.

Balancing the burden of kindling against his side with one arm, he reached for the latch of her doorway, then paused, examining his hands with disgust. He flexed knuckles stained black from shoveling and hauling coal into the burner of the huge stove that heated steam for the first two floors of the estate. Filth from the stables and the gardens embedded beneath his fingernails and settled in the creases and calluses of his palm.

A familiar mortification welled within his chest as he smoothed the hand over his shirt, hoping to buff some of the dirt off like an apple before trying the latch and peering around the door.

Titus loved that—unlike the rest of her family—Honoria slept with all her drapes tied open and the window nearest the honeysuckle vines cracked to allow the scent of the gardens to waft inside. It didn't seem to matter the season or the weather, he'd look up to her window to find it thusly open.

Sometimes he would sing while he worked outside. If he were lucky, the sound would draw her to the window, or at least he fancied it did, when she gazed out over the gardens.

Like the sun, he couldn't look at her for too long.

And she barely ever glanced at him.

Titus told himself if she closed the casement against the sound, he'd never utter another note.

But she hadn't.

It was as if she couldn't bear to be completely shut in. As if she couldn't bring herself to draw the drapes and close the world out.

On this morning, the November chill matched the slate grey of the predawn skies visible through her corner windows. Fingers of ice stole through his vest and thin shirt, prompting him to hurry and warm the room for her.

Shivering inside, he held his breath as he eased the door closed behind him, taking extra care against waking her as she'd been drawn and quiet for a few days and often complained of headaches.

In the dimness, she was little more than a slim outline beneath a mountain of arabesque silk bedclothes, curled with her back to him. Her braid an inky swath against the clean white pillow.

She occupied the second grandest bedroom, her being the eldest and all. The ceiling was tall enough to boast a crystal chandelier that matched the smaller sconces flanking her headboard. More than one wardrobe stood sentinel against the white wainscoting, containing her plethora of garments and gowns, each to be worn at different times of the day or for varied soirees, teas, and other such events unimaginable to someone like him.

She favored gem-bright hues over pastels, and silks over cottons and velvets. With her wealth of ebony hair and eyes so dark it was hard to distinguish pupil from iris, every cut and color flattered her endlessly.

But Titus knew red was her favorite. She wore it most often in every conceivable shade.

In the stillness of the morning, he could hear that her breaths were erratic and uneven, as if she were running in a dream, or struggling with some unseen foe.

On carpets as plush as hers, his feet made no sound as he tiptoed past the foot of a bed so cavernous that it would have swallowed his humble cot in the loft above the mews, three times over.

Was she having a nightmare?

Would it be a kindness to wake her?

Perhaps. But he'd expect to be summarily dismissed for even presuming to do such a thing.

He dawdled over the fire, laying the most perfect blaze ever constructed. Once the flames crackled and popped cheerfully in the hearth, he lingered still, content to simply share the air she breathed.

"Is it burning?"

Her hoarse words nearly startled him out of his own skin.

Titus jumped to his feet, upsetting his kindling basket,

and dropping the poker on the stones with a thunderous clatter.

"The—the fire, miss? Aye. It's burning proper now. It'll warm your bones and no mistake." Compared to her high-born dialect, his Yorkshire accent sounded like ripe gibberish, even to his own ears.

"It's burning me," she complained tightly, the words terse and graveled as if her throat closed over them.

"Miss?" His heart pounded as he approached her side of the bed, then sank at what he found.

Her braid was a tangle, escaped tendrils matted to her slick forehead and temples as if she'd done battle with it all night. Lines of pain crimped her brow and pinched the skin beside her lips thin and white.

She wasn't simply curled against the cold but, more accurately, around herself. As if to protect her torso from pain. Though beads of sweat gathered at her hairline and her upper lip, she shivered intermittently.

It was her eyes, though, that terrified him. Open, but fixed on nothing, not even noting his approach.

"Miss Goode?" he whispered. "Can you—can you hear me?"

Suddenly her limbs became restless as she arched and flailed weakly, shoving her bedcovers away from her body, revealing that she'd clawed her nightdress off sometime during the night.

Honoria Goode was pale in the most normal of circumstances, but her lithe nude limbs were nearly indistinguishable from the white sheets, but for the feverish red flush creeping up her torso, over her breasts, and toward her clavicles.

"It's burning my skin," she croaked, levering herself up on shaking arms. "Everywhere. Put it out, boy, *please*."

Boy. Later, the word would pierce him like a lance.

She made a plaintive sound that sliced his guts open, and made to roll off the bed.

10

"No, miss. You're with fever. Lie still. I'll wake the house." Without thinking, he reached for her shoulders, meaning to keep her in place.

She stunned him by collapsing back to the pillow in a heap of bliss at his touch. "Yes," she sighed, clutching at his hands. "So cold. So...better."

The winter air was frigid and damp this morning and laying the fires had done next to nothing to slake the bone-deep chill from his fingers and toes.

Her skin did, indeed, feel as hot as any flame beneath his palms, leeching whatever comforting cold his hands could offer as she warmed him in kind.

Panic trilled through him, seizing his limbs. As an un-educated boy, he knew very little, but he understood the danger she was in all too well. She *was* burning from the inside out, and if something wasn't done, she'd become just another ghost to haunt the void in his heart where his loved ones used to live.

Snatching up her sheets, he carefully swaddled her enough to keep her from doing herself any harm, before tearing out of the room.

He rang every bell, roused every adult from their beds with frantic intensity. The Baron immediately sent him for their doctor, Preston Alcott. Not wanting to waste the time it took for the old stable master to saddle a horse, Titus ran the several blocks to the doctor's, arriving just as his lungs threatened to burst from the frigid coal-stained air.

Doctor Alcott was still punching his arms into his coat as Titus dragged him down his front stoop in a groggy heap of limbs, and shoved him into a hansom. To save time, he relayed all the details of his interaction with Honoria, noting her feverish behavior, appearance, and answering supplemental questions, such as what she'd had to eat the night before and where she'd traveled to in the past couple of days.

"You are a rather observant lad," the doctor remarked, peering over the rims of his spectacles. It was difficult to distinguish beneath the man's curly russet beard if he was being complimentary or condemning, until Alcott said, "Would that my nurses would be half as detailed as you."

Even though it wasn't his place, upon their arrival, Titus trailed the doctor up the grand staircase and lurked in the hallway, near an oriental vase almost as tall as he was, doing his best to blend with the shadows.

Through Honoria's open door, he watched helplessly as Mrs. Mcgillicutty, the housekeeper, ran a cool cloth over Honoria's face and throat. The Goodes hovered behind her, as if nursing their firstborn was still so beneath them, they needed a servant to do it.

Honoria laid on her back, mummified by her sheets, her lids only half-open now.

Titus thought he might be sick. She'd become so colorless, he might have thought her dead already, but for the slight, rapid rise and fall of her chest.

The doctor shooed them all aside and took only minutes of examination to render the grave verdict. "Baron and Lady Cresthaven, Mrs. Mcgillicutty, have any of you previously suffered from typhoid fever?"

Honoria's mother, an older copy of her dark-haired daughters, recoiled from her bedside. "Certainly not, Doctor. That is an affliction of the impoverished and squalid."

If the doctor had any opinions on her reaction, he kept them to himself. "If that is the case, then I'm going to have to ask you to leave this room. Indeed, it would be safer if you took your remaining children and staff elsewhere until…"

"Until Honoria recovers?" the Baron prompted through his wealth of a mustache.

The doctor gazed down at Honoria with a soft expression bordering on grief.

Titus wanted to scream. To kick at the priceless vase beside him and glory in the destruction, if only to see something as shattered as his heart might be.

"I knew she shouldn't have been allowed to attend Lady Carmichaels's philanthropic event," the Baroness shrilled. "I've always maintained nothing good can come of venturing below Clairview Street."

"Is there anyone else in your house feeling ill, Lady Cresthaven?" the doctor asked as he opened his arms in a gesture meant to shuffle them all toward the door.

"Not that I'm aware of," she answered as she hurried from her daughter's side as if swept up in Alcott's net.

"Two maids," Mrs. Mcgillicutty said around her mistress. "They took to their beds ill last night."

The doctor heaved a long-suffering sigh as they approached the threshold. "Contrary to popular belief, typhoid contamination can happen to the food and drink of anyone at any time. It is true and regrettable that more of this contamination is rampant in the poorer communities, where sanitation is woefully inadequate, but this is a pathogen that does not discriminate based on status."

"Quite so," the Baron agreed in the imperious tone he used when he felt threatened or out of his depth. "We'll leave for the Savoy immediately. Charlotte, get your things."

"I'll need someone to draw your daughter a cool bath and help me lift her into it," the doctor said, his droll intonation never changing. "If you'd inquire through the household about anyone who has been inflicted with typhoid fever in the past—"

"I have done, Doctor." Titus stepped out of the shadows, startling both of the Goodes. "It took my parents and my sister."

Before that moment, Titus hadn't known someone could appear both relieved and grim, but Alcott managed it.

"Absolutely not!" Charlotte Goode was not a large woman, but her staff often complained her voice could reach an octave that could shatter glass and offend dogs. "I'm not having my eldest, the jewel of our family, *handled* by the boy who shovels our coal and horse manure. This is most distressing; Honoria was invited to the Princess's garden party next week as the Viscount Clairmont's special guest!"

Titus lowered his eyes. Not out of respect for the woman, but so she wouldn't see the flames of his rage licking into his eyes.

At this, the doctor actually stomped his foot against the floor, silencing everyone. "Madam, your daughter barely has a chance of lasting the week, and the longer you and your family reside beneath this roof, the more danger your other children are in. Do I make myself clear?"

The Baron, famously pragmatic to the point of ruthlessness, took his wife by the shoulders and steered her away. "We're going," he said.

Without a backward glance at his firstborn.

TIED WITH A BOW

*D*octor Alcott took all of two seconds to dismiss the frantic bustle of the Baron's household, and yanked Titus into Honoria's bedroom before shutting them in. "Where is the bathroom?"

Titus pointed to a door through which the adjoining bathroom also shared a door with the nursery on the other side.

"Does the tub have a tap directly to it, or is it necessary to haul water from the kitchens?"

"It's a pump tap, sir, but I've only just started the boiler and that only pipes hot water to the kitchens and the first floor."

"That's sufficient." The doctor divested himself of his suit coat and abandoned it to a chair before undoing the links on his cuffs. "Now I need you to fill the bath with cool water, not cold, do you understand? We need to combat that fever, but if the water is freezing, it'll cause her to shiver and raise her temperature."

"I'll go to the kitchens and have them boil a pan just to make sure it inn't icy."

The man reached into his medical bag and extracted an opaque lump. "First, young man, you will take this an-

15

KERRIGAN BYRNE

tiseptic soap and scrub your hands until even the dirt from beneath your fingernails is gone."

"Yes, sir."

It took a veritable eternity for the water to boil, but it seemed he needed every moment of that to scrub the perpetual filth from his hands. Once his skin was pink and raw with nary a speck, he filled two buckets as full as he could carry and hauled the boiling-hot water up the stairs.

The Baron and his wife swept by him on their way down. "We mustn't let on it's typhoid," he was saying as his wife plunged her hands into an ermine muff.

"You're right, of course," the Baroness agreed. "What assumptions would people make about our household? Perhaps influenza would be more apropos?"

"Yes, capital suggestion."

Titus firmly squelched the impulse to dump the scalding water over the Goodes' collective heads, and raced to the bathroom, his arms aching from the load. He instantly threw the lock against the nursery as he heard the high-pitched, fearful questions the young twins barraged their governess with on the other side of the door. He plugged the tub's drain and turned the tap. Cringing at the frigidity of the water, he balanced the temperature as best he could.

That done, he returned to Honoria's room in time to see the doctor, clad only in his trousers and shirtsleeves rolled to the elbows, bending over a nude Honoria with his hands upon her stomach, spanning above her belly button.

Even in her catatonic state, she produced a whimper of distress that fell silent when the doctor's hands moved lower, his fingers digging into the flesh above her hip bone, on the line where her pale skin met a whorl of ebony hair.

An instantaneous primal rage surged through Titus at

16

the sight. With an animalistic sound he'd never made before, Titus lunged around the bed and shoved the doctor away from her.

Alcott stumbled into the nightstand, upsetting a music box and her favorite hairbrush.

Titus threw the bedclothes back over Nora, snarling at the doctor as he placed his body as a shield against the much larger man. "You keep your fucking filthy hands from her."

Rather than becoming guilty or defensive, the doctor's shock flared into irritation, and then, as he examined Titus, it melted into comprehension. He adjusted his spectacles and advanced a few steps. "Listen to me, lad. I am a man, yes, and she is a lady. But in this room, I am *only* a doctor. To me, this is the body of a dying human. I must examine her."

Titus narrowed his eyes in suspicion, wondering if this man took him for a dupe. "You don't have to touch her... *there.* Not so close to—"

Alcott interrupted him crisply. "Though I am convinced of my initial diagnosis, I would do her a disservice if I didn't rule out all other possibilities. Internally, many maladies can produce these symptoms, and therefore palpating the stomach will often help me make certain she is not in other danger. You have an organ, the appendix, right here." He indicated low to the right of his torso, almost to his groin. "If it becomes swollen or perforated, it will spread fever and infection through the blood. If this were the case with Miss Goode, an immediate operation would be required, or she'd be dead before noon."

Noon? Titus swallowed around a dry lump, peering over his shoulder at her lovely face made waxen by a sheen of sweat.

"Your protection of her is commendable. But it is my duty to keep this girl alive," the doctor prodded, venturing even closer now. "That obligation takes precedence in my thoughts and my deeds, over anything so banal as modesty, as it must in yours now while you help me get her into the bath. Do you think you are capable of that?"

Titus nodded, even as a fist of dread and pain knotted in his stomach.

The doctor reached out and patted his shoulder. "Good. Now help me get the sheet beneath her and we'll use it as a sort of sling."

She fought them as they lowered her—sheet and all—into the bath, before suddenly settling into it with a sigh of surrender. After a few fraught moments, her breath seemed to come easier. The wrinkles of pain in her forehead smoothed out a little as her onyx lashes relaxed down over her flushed cheeks.

Alcott, his movements crisp and efficient, abandoned the room, only to return to administer a tincture she seemed to have trouble swallowing.

"What's that?" Titus queried, eyeing the bottle with interest.

"Thymol. Better known as thyme camphor. It has anti-pathogenic properties that will attack the bacteria in her stomach, giving her greater chance of survival."

"The doctor gave us all naphthalene," Titus remembered. "It helped with the fever, but...then they all got so much worse." The memory thrummed a chord of despondency in his chest with such a pulsating ache, he had to press his hand to his sternum to quiet it.

Alcott snorted derisively, his skin mottling beneath his beard. "Naphthalene is more a poison than a medicine, and while it's less expensive and more readily available, it is also little better than shoving mothballs into your family's mouth and calling it a cure. I'd very much like a word with this so-called physician."

Would that Titus had known before. He could have perhaps asked for this...thymol. "I don't know why I didn't get so sick as them. I did everything I could for their fevers. Yarrow tea and cold ginger. I couldn't lift them into a bath, I was a boy then, but I kept cold compresses on their heads and camphor and mustard on their chests."

Alcott's features arranged themselves with such compassion, Titus couldn't look at him without a prick of tears threatening behind his eyes. "You did admirably, lad. Sometimes, despite our best efforts, death wins the battle and we doctors are defeated."

To assuage both his curiosity and his inescapable anxiety, Titus questioned the doctor about bacteria, pathogens, medications, dosages, appendixes—and any other organs that might arbitrarily perforate—until Alcott deemed that Honoria had spent long enough in the water.

It was difficult to maintain the sort of clinical distance Doctor Alcott seemed capable of as they maneuvered her back to the bed, and dried and dressed her in a clean night rail. Titus did his best to avoid looking where he ought not to, touching her bare skin as little as possible.

But he knew his fingertips wouldn't forget the feel of her, even though it dishonored them both to remember.

The doctor left her in Titus's care while he went to administer thymol and instruction to the maids, both of whom were afflicted with the same malady but not advanced with high fevers or this worrisome torpor.

Once alone, Titus retrieved the hairbrush and, with trembling hands and exacting thoroughness, undid the matted mess that had become her braid. He smoothed the damp strands and fanned them over the pillow as he gently worked out the tangles. The texture was like silk against his rough skin, and he allowed himself to indulge in the pleasure of the drying strands sifting in the divots between his fingers. Then, he plaited it as he sometimes did the horses' tails when they had to be moved *en masse* to the country.

He even tied the end with a ribbon of burgundy, thinking she might approve.

His efforts, of course, were nothing so masterful as Honoria's maid's, but he was examining the finished product with something like satisfaction when the appearance of Doctor Alcott at his side gave him a start.

The doctor, a man of maybe forty years, was looking down at him from eyes still pink with exhaustion, as if he'd not slept before being roused so early. "We'll leave her to slumber until her next dose of thymol. Here, I'll draw the drapes against the morning."

"No." Titus stood, reaching out a staying hand for the doctor. "She prefers the windows and drapes open. She likes the breeze from the garden, even in the winter."

The doctor nodded approvingly. "It's my opinion fresh air is best for an ailing patient." He moved to put a hand on her forehead and take her pulse, seeming encouraged by the results. That finished, he turned to Titus, assessing him with eyes much too shrewd and piercing for a boy used to living his life largely unseen.

"She means something to you, boy?"

She meant *everything* to him. But of course, he could not say that.

"Titus."

"Pardon?"

"My name is Titus Conleith."

The doctor gave a curt nod. "Irish?"

"My father was, but my mum was from Yorkshire, where they worked the factories. We were sent here when my dad was elevated to a foreman in a steel company. But the well was bad, and typhoid took them all three months later."

Alcott made a sound that might have been sympathetic. "And how'd you come to be employed in the household of a Baron?"

Titus shrugged, increasingly uncomfortable beneath the older man's interrogation. "I saved old Mr. Fick, the stable master, from being crushed by a runaway carriage one time. He gave me the job here to keep me from having to go back to the workhouse, as his joints are getting too rheumatic to do what he used to. Besides, no orphanage would take in a boy old enough to make trouble."

"I see. Have you any schooling?"

Titus eyed him warily. "I have some numbers and letters. What's it to you?"

"You've a good mind for what I do. A good stomach for it, as well. I've a surgery off Basil Street, in Knightsbridge. Do you know where that is?"

"Aye."

He clasped his hands behind his back, looking suddenly regimental. "If Mr. Fick can spare you a few nights a week, I want you to visit me there. We can talk about your future."

"I will," Titus vowed, something sparking inside of him that his worry for Honoria wouldn't allow to ignite into full hope.

The three days he sat at her side were both the best and worst of his life.

He told her tales about the horses' antics as he melted chips of ice into her mouth. He monitored her for spikes of fever and kept her cool with damp cloths and linens packed with ice. The doctor even let him dose her with the thymol and look after most of her necessities when the maids took a turn for the worse.

He begged her to live.

All the while, he crooned the Irish tune his father used to sing to his mother on the nights when they drank a bit too much ale and danced a reel like young lovers, across their dingy old floor.

Black is the color of my true love's hair,
Her lips are like some roses fair,
She's the sweetest smile and the gentlest hands,
I love the ground whereon she stands.

HE BARELY ATE OR SLEPT UNTIL THE FOURTH NIGHT, AFTER she'd swallowed several spoonsful of beef bone broth, the deep sounds of her easier breaths lulling him to nap in the chair by her bed. Alcott had roused him with the good news that her fever had broken, and had then ordered him to wash and change clothing and sleep in the guest room nearby.

A commotion woke him thirteen hours later. Without thinking, Titus lurched out of bed and scrambled down the hall. Skidding to a halt, he narrowly avoided crashing into the Baron's back.

Every soul in the Goode family gathered around Honoria's bed, blocking her from view. Prudence, Felicity, and Mercy all chattered at the same time, and it was the happy sound of their cadence that told him he had nothing to fear.

Titus squelched a spurt of possession, stopping just short of shoving in and around them to see what was going on. This moment didn't belong to them, it belonged to him.

She belonged to him.

"Young Mr. Conleith, there you are." Doctor Alcott, a tall man, stood at the head of the bed next to his patient, who was still blocked from Titus's view. "Miss Goode, you and your family owe this young lad a debt of gratitude. It is largely due to his tireless efforts that you survived."

They all turned to look at him, clearing the visual pathway to her.

With an ecstatic elation, Titus drank in the sight of

Honoria sitting up on her own. She was still ashen and wan, her eyes heavy-lidded and her lips without color.

And yet, the most beautiful sight he'd laid his eyes upon.

Her fingers worried at the burgundy ribbon in her hair, stroking it as if drawing comfort from it.

Was it his imagination, or did a dash of peach color her cheeks at the sight of him?

He already knew he was red as a beet, swamped in the blush now creeping up his collar.

"Thank you," she whispered.

Every word he knew crowded in his throat, choking off a reply.

"Yes," the Baron chuffed, taking his shoulder and firmly steering him backwards. "Expect our gratitude in remuneration, boy. I'll call for you to come to my office tomorrow to discuss the details. There's a good lad."

The door shut in his face, and he stared at it for an incomprehensible moment. From the other side, the Baroness's voice grated as she asked the doctor if Honoria might be well enough to attend the garden party at the palace three days hence.

Titus dropped his head against the door and closed his eyes.

She'd looked right at him. Had *seen* him for the first time. Did she remember any of the previous days? Had she heard anything he'd said to her? Sung to her?

She'd thanked him.

And he'd said nothing. His one chance to actually speak to her and he'd choked.

And then he'd been shut out like the inconvenience he was. To them, the Goodes, he was still a nobody. Nothing. They would never think about him after today unless the dog shat upon the carpets and someone needed to clean it up.

Would she? Would she come to him? Had she noticed him, truly? Not as a servant or a savior but as himself...

One question haunted him as he dragged his feet down the hallway, back to the mews, his hand curling over the memory of her skin.

Would he ever get to touch her again?

"*I* do believe someone is dead beneath your greenhouse," Amanda Pettifer said with no real concern as she pulled the curtain back from the carriage window. "That's quite a structure for merely a Baron's home. Why, it's as long as your stable walls."

Honoria Goode didn't miss Amanda's latent jab at their rank. As the daughter of a viscount, she needed, upon occasion, to put them in their place. It wasn't the most pleasant virtue for a friend to have, but neither was it uncommon among their class.

"Let me see!" Prudence lunged over Amanda's lap to peer out the carriage window as they clopped in beneath the mews. "Holy Moses! You're right. A man's legs are sticking out from beneath as if the structure landed right on him. What if he drowned in that puddle of muck he's in? Someone should do something, Nora! Oh…no…wait. The legs are moving. All is well. At least, I *think* it is."

"I'm glad our welcome party isn't a corpse." Secretly pleased that her sister Pru still used the nickname she'd gleaned at finishing school, Nora marked her page and closed her book. She'd never liked the name Honoria. It was stolid and plain, belonging more to a nun or a suffragist than a debutante. Nora sounded much more so-phisticated, she thought. Tidier, even.

Though Amanda Pettifer was Nora's age at twenty, she and Prudence—almost three years their junior at seventeen—were thick as thieves. Likely, because they both shared a penchant for mischief and misbehavior.

They'd all bundled into the carriage from the Green Street Station, anxious to arrive home. Nora's coming out ball was in three days, and there was so much to be done. She couldn't help but become almost overwrought with anxiety at the thought.

The carriage trundled to a stop in their Mayfair court-yard as she swept aside the curtains to see what all the hullabaloo was about.

Along the wall of their extensive stables, tucked into the square behind their grand row house, Mrs. Fick's glass and wrought-iron greenhouse glinted with the colors of the setting sun.

Indeed, sprawled in a shallow mud puddle from a pit dug beneath the foundation, were two long male legs clad in filthy trousers. As the girls all watched, the legs bent and splayed indecently as mud-caked hands appeared and clasped the underside of the structure. Then, with a serpentine struggle, the entire body of a man shimmied on his back from beneath.

Before sitting up, he reached back under and retrieved several work tools.

"Good lord, Nora, he's all but naked," Prudence gasped.

The young man hauled himself to his feet and smoothed his muddy hair before scraping some of the muck from his torso and flicking it onto the ground.

Amanda's buttercream lace fan snapped open with a frenetic rip. "My," she exclaimed huskily. "He's built exactly like that statue of Ares in the Louvre."

26

Nora barely heard their remarks, so arrested was she by the sight of him.

Amanda had the right of it. His figure could have been sculpted by the hands of a master. His jaw chiseled granite and his smooth sinewy torso shaped from marble. He was long-limbed and slender, his shoulders round and his arms corded with lean muscle. The flat discs of his chest gave way to grooved ribs and an abdomen so defined she could count the individual muscles, six in all.

She'd never seen a man like this in the flesh. Sculptors were a talented lot, to be sure, but they worked in clay and stone. A cold, lifeless modality in comparison. It could not begin to capture the jaw-dropping glint of golden skin. The line of intriguing hair disappearing into his trousers. Nor the peaks and shadows created by the grooves of muscle as he moved and flexed beneath the disappearing sunlight.

The moment the footman opened the door, Amanda accepted his hand and all but leapt out of the carriage to whistle at the workman. "You seem to have lost your clothing, sir," she taunted.

His head snapped up as Prudence followed Amanda out of the carriage and tittered, "Mr. Fick will have to turn the garden hose on you, before all that mud dries you into a statue."

"Let it dry, I say." Amanda made a show of leering over at him, assessing him from head to toe. "Store him in a museum. I'd pay admittance to see that work of art *regularly*."

"Amanda! What if someone heard you?" Prudence put a lace-gloved hand over her friend's unruly mouth, though they were both giggling uncontrollably.

"What do I care?" Amanda grappled her hand away and flounced toward the door, her cream ruffled skirts fanning out behind her. "I'm to marry a short, pudgy lord who owns half of Cheshire, but I will always be an appreciator of excellent artisan workmanship. They don't make men like that in our class, do they? More's the pity."

Nora was about to deliver a sharp word of reprimand when Mr. Fick, the spindly, white-haired stable master tossed a balled-up cotton shirt at the lad, hitting him square in the chest. "Oi! Titus! Make yourself decent; you're offending the ladies!"

"He *really* isn't," Amanda said huskily.

Turning, the kindly Mr. Fick bowed as Nora was the last to step down from the carriage. "Miss Goode, Miss Goode, Miss Pettifer, welcome back."

"Thank you, Mr. Fick, it's lovely to see you!" Prudence greeted with all her usual cheer.

Nora couldn't bring herself to speak, gaping as she was in slack-jawed amazement.

That was Titus Conleith?

He touched the shirt as little as possible as he held it away from his mud-covered skin. Shifting restlessly, his features arranged themselves into an uncomfortable frown that lanced Nora through with mortification.

"Pardon me, ladies. Mr. Fick, I'll test the piping to see if the water pressure is returned." His voice was deep and graveled, the register low enough that Nora had to strain to hear it. He barely gave them a curt nod, opened the door, and escaped into the long greenhouse.

"Let's go and surprise Mama and the Pater," Prudence crowed, peeling her hat away from the onyx curls that matched Nora's own. "Then I'll show Amanda to her room and hopefully supper will be ready soon. I'm positively faint with hunger. Are you coming, Nora?"

"In a moment," she replied, barely noticing the girls' giggling retreat.

Between the rows and shelves of vegetables, herbs, spices, and flowers tended by Mrs. Fick's magical green thumb, she could catch glimpses of Titus through the panes of glass as he drifted deeper into the greenhouse.

"Watch your pretty shoes, there, miss." Mr. Fick motioned to the puddle nearly large enough to be a pond. "We installed irrigation pipes into the greenhouse last week, and already one of them sprung a leak. Titus's been at fixing it all day. Knowing you, you'll be wanting to greet the horses before the people," he said affectionately. "I think old Cleo is back there waiting for you."

That drew a genuine smile from her. She did, indeed, prefer horses to people in almost all cases. "Yes, thank you."

He blinked over at the greenhouse, then cast the retreating girls a look of veiled disapproval before taking himself off toward the servants' entrance.

Nora waited for him to disappear inside before skirting the puddle, lifting the hem of her powder blue gown, and hopping onto the landing of the greenhouse to slip inside.

Moist air fragrant with loamy soil and herbs suffused Nora's lungs. She breathed it in, longing for the country. The sound of running water drew her past strawberries and asparagus, basil, rosemary, coriander, thyme, even a tomato vine struggling to find the sun.

Toward the rear of the structure, fresh flowers bared themselves shamelessly, overgrowing the pathway and impeding her view. Nora had to lift a few fern fronds to duck beneath them.

She found Titus surrounded by a bevy of hanging plants, bent over a drain as he scrubbed the dirt from his hair and back with the pump Mrs. Fick used to water her plants.

"Leak is patched, I'm sure of it, Mr. Fick," he said, shaking his hair like a dog. "Whoever installed that pipe must have been drunk or blind." He dropped the hose to the drain and ran his hands over his face, swiping water and grit away from his eyes. "Will you hand over my shirt?"

Even after his many years in the city, he had not lost those lovely long vowels of Yorkshire.

Nora retrieved his nearly white shirt from where it splayed over a bush that had been clipped ruthlessly short, and held it over to him. She had the odd desire to keep it captive, or do something ridiculous, like hold it to her nose and test the scent. "Here you are."

He didn't straighten so much as jump, his wet hair releasing a little arc of spray that barely missed her. It was the color of dark sand after the lap of a wave had been called out to sea, and it hung to his eyes in spiked gathers that dripped onto his skin.

The effect made his symmetrical features more powerful, somehow, causing the bones to etch dramatic angles that she knew would become even more stark and compelling when he was an older man.

He slicked his hair back with frantic motions before running his hand over his eyes and face once more, as if clearing the water from them would dissolve her from his sight.

The movements did things to the muscles of his arms and chest, that transfixed her into a mute sort of appreciation that should have shamed them both. He was cold, she noted. His nipples pebbled and gooseflesh chased across his skin.

What a constitution one must have, to bathe with the irrigation hose, the water pumped from frigid wells and aquifers.

"Honoria." Her name manifested in a throaty whisper, then he winced. "That is, Miss Goode." Instead of stepping closer, he bent at the waist and snatched the shirt hanging from her lax fingers.

She'd almost dropped it whilst gawking.

"My friends call me Nora," she said inanely before cursing herself for a ninny. He'd not be allowed to address her thusly. They were not friends because they were not equals.

He threaded his arms into his shirt without even bothering to dry himself, heedless, it seemed, of the fact that his trousers were still filthy, thus rendering a clean shirt obsolete.

Propriety dictated, however, that he protect his modesty—and more importantly hers—before his own meager wardrobe.

He didn't look at her as he fumbled with the buttons, his eyes cast down at the drain. "Is there something I can do for you?"

She shook her head, suddenly feeling silly and...oddly short. The last time she'd seen him, she'd looked down at him. Now, he could likely rest his chin on top of her head.

Nora did her best to stammer out what she had come to say. "Y-you are owed an apology. Amanda and Pru—well, I suppose we all were being disrespectful just now by staring and carrying on. I'm sorry if we embarrassed you. It's only that, we've had an arduous journey back from a terrible few years at finishing school and we're all feeling a bit spirited. I suppose, what with the ball upcoming and such..." She trailed away, knowing she was babbling, and realizing how weak and awful her excuses made her sound.

She could cheerfully murder Amanda right now.

And then, perhaps not, because she had a reason to be alone. With him. She had the image of his musculature etched into her memory to take out and appreciate at her own leisure.

Titus Conleith.

She didn't used to think the grand name suited him

31

when he was a small and skinny boy with huge, hungry golden eyes. His gaze had always reminded her of Ramses, their German shepherd puppy, when he begged at the kitchen door for scraps.

But, like Ramses, Titus was no pup now. Though his eyes were still hungry.

Piercing but evasive.

"Anyway," she said, stroking at the leaf of a dangling ivy plant, if only to have something to fidget with. "I hope you're not cross. Most young ladies are unused to the sight of... well..." She gestured in his general direction, lamenting the disappearance of his smooth chest as he buttoned toward his neck.

"I'm not cross, miss."

She could feel her brow crimping with worry. It was impossible to tell from the tone of his voice if he was merely being polite. Perhaps he felt as though he could not convey his affrontedness because her father was his employer. She disliked that thought immensely.

"It wasn't well done of us to stare, let alone for anyone to make a comment. It was uncouth and rude and—"

"You can stare." His eyes met hers then, the golden gaze intense and inescapable, though his sober features never changed from intractable. "I wouldn't stop you."

The way he was looking at her now, made her very aware of the cinch of her corset and how little air she was allowing into her lungs.

She did stare, then, rather dumbly, trying to dissect the meaning beneath his words. He wouldn't stop her because he *could* not? Because she was his superior? Or he would not stop her... because he desired her to look at him?

Because he wanted her to appreciate what she saw?

Because she had.

She *did*.

The air thickened between them, taking on the muffled, expectant quality of the atmosphere right before a thunderstorm. The hairs on her body lifted, shivered, as if anticipating a lightning strike.

"Nora!" Mercy's screech broke the spell of the moment as her little sister exploded into the greenhouse. "Nora, you're home!" The gangly, golden-haired girl barreled into her, cinching small, surprisingly strong arms about her waist in a breath-stealing hug.

Felicity, Mercy's twin, wasn't far behind, though she waited patiently for her turn. "Hullo, Titus," she said, adjusting her spectacles as if looking at him blinded her a little.

Nora understood the feeling.

"Oi, Miss Felicity." His voice softened when he spoke to her sister, and the effect was something like velvet rasping over silk.

"I've almost finished *Chemistry, Meteorology, and the Production of Vapour*," Felicity announced. "If I return it this evening before you go, might you ask Doctor Alcott for another?"

Doctor Alcott? Nora wondered. Were they still in touch after—?

"Have you now, with those big words and everything?" Titus's eyes crinkled at the edges in a most alluring way when he smiled. "Clever girl, you are. I think Alcott has one on alchemical preservation I could bring you. It is all about mummies."

"I *love* mummies." Felicity blushed to the roots of her blond hair, and Nora realized that whenever the word *clever* was used regarding Felicity in their household, it wasn't complimentary. One would be pressed to find a volume that wasn't religious or political in nature. The Goode girls were not allowed vulgar modern literature. In fact, she should hide her novel before she went inside.

At the thought of returning home, another long-held anxiety floated to the surface like a poorly weighted drowning victim. Per her father's insistence, her ball gown wasn't cut to style. High necks were for everyday gowns, and evening wear went so far as to slide below the shoulders.

And yet hers was buttoned to the chin.

Everyone was going to laugh.

Suddenly a memory blew across her mind like an autumnal gust.

Titus. His hands at her neck, doing or... undoing buttons. *Her* buttons... brushing soft, cool cloths over her neck and chest.

She swallowed, her fingers lifting to tug at her lace collar.

Mercy released her waist only to seize hold of her hand. "Papa sent us to fetch you, Nora. After you meet with him, you *must* come and have tea with us in the nursery. I've written a play and Pru said she'll be the boy but only today as you'll be too busy with your blasted ball after that."

"Don't let nanny hear you say blast," Nora warned, too charmed to truly scold her beloved sister.

"There's kissing in the play," Felicity said with a scandalized look up at Titus. "But we put our hands over our mouths."

"Come on." Mercy tugged. "Do hurry!"

"Good afternoon, Titus," Felicity said with a prim curtsy.

He nodded his head at them each in turn. "And a good afternoon to you, Miss Felicity, Miss Mercy." He bowed to them both with all the starched sobriety of a general before turning to her and inclining his head. "Miss Goode."

As Nora allowed herself to be towed to the house by two cherubic ten-year-old tugboats, she couldn't help but notice he'd called her *Miss Goode*. As he should have...and yet...

He'd enjoyed a bit of familiarity with the girls. Why not her? Could she insist he call her Nora? What would the word sound like now that his voice had altered so profoundly?

It was all she could think about for the rest of the day.

THE BALL

N ora hated every moment she shared with
Michael Leventhorpe, the heir to the Marquess of Blandbury. He was not only a fool, but a bully
and a rake.

She didn't like him.

She didn't want him.

And she was left with *no choice* but to marry him.

Which was why he'd been allowed to conduct her
away from the stifling ball, out onto the balcony. He
swept her to the darkest corner, where the stone col-
umns of the banister overlooked the garden. The
pathway was dimly lit for the occasion by decorative an-
tique braziers that brought to mind Shakespeare's
London.

Though most of the girls considered Blandbury handsome, nay, the catch of the season, Nora categorically dis-
agreed. He was a big buffoon of a man, sporting and solid
with pale hair and skin so white she could see some of the
blue veins beneath the skin of his eyes. For some reason,
she could stare at little else, all the while berating herself
for being too critical of appearance.

She would never have given Blandbury a second
glance if it hadn't been for her father's welcome home

three days prior, delivered with a stern edict that'd stolen any light from her heart.

Clarence Goode, Baron Cresthaven, had always cowed her. But never so much as when she was made to stand before the desk he'd mounted on a massive dais in his study, simply so he could look down at people as if from behind the Queen's Bench in court. He was a veritable force of nature, tall and broad, but not in the way that Titus had become. Not with that lean strength and effortless grace. Her father was a rotund man with the dimensions of a whiskey barrel and the hands of a cooper, rather than a nobleman.

He had stared down at her with a disapproval she hadn't yet earned, regarding her with an assessment any ewe at auction might still find insulting.

"Every man wishes for a boy to take on his legacy," he'd begun, stroking at his impressive mustache as if delivering a homily of great import. "Since your mother and I were not so blessed with an heir, that doesn't change the nature of the necessity. Were you a son, you'd be groomed to take over my title and my company. I'd apprentice you to the shipping trade and school you in politics so you would be a pinnacle of the Tories." His eyes had taken on a dreamy cast then, as if this was a pleasant fiction he visited often in daydreams.

Nora hadn't been able to contain a sneeze, and the sound brought his disapproving gaze squarely back to her. He made it immediately clear her sinuses were not the only part of her body he currently found offensive. "As you are a woman, you haven't the constitution nor the intellect for such matters, but that doesn't mean you don't have a duty to uphold to your family as firstborn."

Nora hadn't known what to say to that, so she kept her own council. Brevity wasn't among her father's repertoire, so she settled in for a lengthy diatribe.

"If our legacy is to advance, then you must marry well,

as you know. I am spending a veritable fortune on this upcoming ball to put you out in society, and it is incumbent upon you to make a match in your first season, to make way for Prudence. You and your sister shouldn't be coming out so close together, but I suppose that couldn't be helped what with the entire year it took you to gain your strength after your contracting that dastardly fever."

He said this as if fevers were an affliction of the morally degenerate, and indeed, they'd treated her as such for quite some time after her illness.

Perhaps if she hadn't collapsed at the garden party she'd been forced to attend at Buckingham Palace, against the doctor's wishes, she'd have not been so thusly berated.

Her father continued, picking up a pen and opening a folder to study its contents as if the conversation was not important enough to keep his complete attention. "With your charm and beauty, and your competitive dowry, you could snag a Duke if you set your cap to one. There being a marked shortage of marriageable Dukes, I've been talking to the Marquess of Blandbury regarding his son, Michael. It is understood between his father and me, that you will have a proposal at next month's end after no fewer than four social outings with him."

At that, her stomach had lurched, and she'd had to stabilize herself by gripping the high-backed chair she had not been invited to sit in. "But, Papa…how can I be all but promised before I've even had a chance to—"

He stood then, startling her into silence. "You've always been an amenable girl, Honoria. Something I've admired in you. Don't let us disappoint now." He'd moved to the window to stare out over his view of the West End. "With the Marquess as an ally, I could finally clinch the support of the Home Secretary and get my hands on the Metropolitan Police Commissioner position. That done, I'd run the most powerful organized force in the Empire that isn't military."

And that's what it was all about to him.

Power. Prestige. Clout.

She'd be bargained away so her father could play at having a force of minions that would make him feel as though the city belonged to him.

And her buyer was *this* incomparable idiot who hadn't so much as allowed her a word in edgewise for going on ten minutes now.

Nora took in a breath as deep as her constricting peach gown would allow, and tried to listen to what the braggart was saying. Something about what he and his awful society of Oxford friends did to prank the unsuspecting acquaintances of their parents.

He talked too loudly with irritating animation, his eyes alight with self-satisfaction. "You see, it's not stealing, what we do. It's merely a lark. We don't take jewels or silver, because what's the fun in that? We all have plenty of our own, and often such items won't be missed for days or weeks. However, the lads and I pilfer small portraits or love letters, bank notices or diaries. You know, things that are impossible to replace. Then, we sit back and watch the mayhem ensue. One time, Lady Birmingham sacked her entire household!"

He brayed with laughter while Nora's insides twisted.

"That's...horrible," she gasped.

"Nah." He waved his hand in front of his face as if batting away her rebuke. "It's harmless mostly."

"Not if people are losing their positions. That's how they make their living. How they feed their families."

He rolled his eyes. "They'll find another. Who wants to be a servant, anyhow?"

She stared at him, aghast, before finding her voice. "I'm sure no one fantasizes about a life in servitude, but as you're aware, it's a vocation of distinction to work in a noble house. Not to mention a far sight better for many than the dangerous work at the factories, and—"

"Oh, *please* don't tell me you're one of those people in the *ton* who fancy themselves a *liberal*," he sneered, leaning his hip on the banister.

"I don't know what I am," she replied honestly. "I merely fail to see how being so unkind is considered entertaining."

Rather than allow her rebuke to riffle him, he leaned closer, his pale blue eyes darkening with lurid notions. "I'd be kind to you, if you'd let me."

Suddenly she was very aware that her side of the railing abutted a wall, and that no one could see them out here unless they came through the doors and turned in their direction. "Oh. Well that's—"

He leaned closer. "I'd be downright generous...if you'd return the favor."

She cleared a gather of nerves from her throat. "I can't possibly know what you mean."

His lip quirked, but not in the direction she thought it would. "Don't play coy. Not with me. If we're to be married, then everything is permissible." His step toward her felt like an advance, and she retreated in kind, bumping into the wall behind her.

"Are we not supposed to see each other four more times than this?" she reminded him, feeling very cornered. She glanced to the side, meaning to slip away from the wall and dash back inside where they might find someone lingering in the hall if they were lucky. "We've only just met."

He leaned in to brace one hand next to her head, cutting off her path of escape. "I've danced with you twice. Our engagement is all but announced."

Her thoughts began to race, pinging about like a trapped bird looking for escape but doing nothing but crashing into walls. "But I—wouldn't it do to wait until—?"

He didn't kiss her so much as he smashed his mouth

to hers with such force, their teeth met. As she opened her lips to protest, his tongue punched past them, filling her entire mouth and causing her to gag.

His lips were wet and salty, still flavored of the fish they'd had at the banquet, which caused her own meal to rise up her esophagus in revolt.

She broke the kiss by wrenching her head to the side, and he followed her, pressing his mouth to her cheek, breathing hot air against her flesh as he sought to reclaim the kiss.

His weight was crushing, and it seemed as if all the air available to her in the world was his moist, fetid inescapable breath.

"I don't think we should," she said weakly.

"Who gives a damn about should?" he said against her skin, his hands resting on her hips. "This moment is ours, Nora. You're the most beautiful catch of the season and you're *mine*."

She *hated* the way he said that word. The possession in it disgusted her, and still she did her best to remain calm. She'd actually been taught in finishing school how to possibly discourage such advances. What had they said? When men are ruled by their baser natures, appeal to their higher intellect. Remind them they are better.

"We're not engaged, Michael," she said in a beseeching whisper. "If I were caught like this, I'd be ruined."

He scoffed. "I'd still marry you. My father needs your dowry for his estate. Make me a happy man now, and I'll make you a marchioness."

"Please," she whispered. "Don't—"

His mouth caught hers again, cutting off her words. His tongue invaded as tears sprung to her eyes. Hands roamed up and down her waist, his hips pressing her to the side, forcing her against the banister until it bit into her thigh.

Panic gripped her, clawing at her skin. What were her

41

options? To allow him to do this to her or to make a reputation-shredding scene. He was going to be her husband... but how far did he expect to go tonight?

Was this what intimacy was going to be like with him? Forever?

A soft, low growl emanated from the shadows.

And then Michael was gone.

In the time it took for her to gasp a breath into her starving lungs, Titus Conleith had thrown the future Marquess of Blandbury onto the ground and imprisoned him there by grinding his heel against the man's jaw.

In different circumstances, Nora might have found the sight of the boy's cheek squished between Titus's shoe and the ground rather humorous as his body flopped about.

But at the moment, she was too distressed and astonished to ever imagine laughing again.

"Miss Goode said no," Titus informed him with a lethal calm she found more terrifying than if he'd snarled or roared.

"All right. All right, man. Let me up!" Blandbury's voice cracked when Titus's heel ground his face further into the flagstone. His golden eyes glittered with a dangerous intent, as if he considered popping the man's entire head like a ripe melon.

"No." Nora rushed forward and took his arm. "Please don't. Not tonight; it would ruin everything."

His features became still as stone, but a conflagration blazed in those tiger eyes.

It could have blistered her skin if he stared at her for long.

However, at her behest, he took his shoe off the boy's jaw and even lifted Blandbury to his feet, going so far as to brush a smudge off his dinner jacket.

The lord's features mottled with rage. "You're only a *footman*? You dare to put your hands on me?"

Titus appeared unaffected, bringing his nose level with her aggressor's. "You put your hands where they didn't belong first, remember. That deserved an answer."

This time, it was Michael who took a step in retreat. "It is *you* who'll answer for this, the both of you!" He smoothed down his mussed hair and pulled at the lapels of his jacket with anxious, jerky movements as he backed toward the door. "The engagement is off, you hear me? A complete and utter fantasy, thinking to marry so far beneath me. I'll ruin you." He jabbed a finger at Titus, who'd positioned himself in between the furious lord and Nora. "And *you*. You'll be stricken from every decent household in the Empire. You'll die of some god-awful lung disease in the factories. Or worse, the workhouse."

"Marquess of Blandbury?" Clad in a footman's livery, Titus lifted a white-gloved hand to tap his chin as if re-calling a memory. "Isn't it well understood that your fa-ther is dying of cancer?"

Michael's complexion deepened from mottled to pur-ple. "You don't deserve to say his bloody name you—"

Titus's head cocked to the side. "Is it cancer, though? Or syphilis? What would they think, the Tories, about a man who can't abstain from syphilitic whores? What would the papers say?"

At that, Michael blanched, and Nora was again re-pelled by a man whose skin was so reactive to his every emotion. "How do you—where did you find out?"

"What matters is what I'll do with the information. Which is nothing if you apologize to Miss Goode, go to the washroom to sort yourself out, and—after thanking the Baron and his wife for their hospitality—get the fuck out of this house. Because you're right about one thing..." Titus prowled forward, his arm bent behind his back in the posture of a solicitous footman, which made his words land with all the more gravitas as they slid into the night. "There's no *hope* of a wedding, but I know they can arrange a funeral even without a body."

Nora watched with queer, horrific fascination as Michael struggled to breathe. He just stood there, saying nothing until Titus feinted a threatening lunge forward.

"I'm sorry!" he cried. "I—I apologize. I shan't touch you again."

Nora didn't forgive him, of course, but she nodded, if only to release him from their company so he could scamper down the hall.

Once he'd gone, she was seized by a bout of intense vertigo, feeling as if the floor beneath her had become a small sea craft tossed by waves. She collapsed onto a stone bench, not certain her legs could take her weight for much longer.

The repercussions of this would be dire. Her father was going to be *so* angry, and that frightened her a little, but not so much as the tongue just shoved down her throat.

Repulsed by the memory, Nora wiped at her mouth with the back of her glove. Only when it came away damp did she realize tears now streaked down her cheeks in hot rivulets.

A handkerchief was pressed into her fingers, and she looked up to see Titus staring down at her with that alarmingly indecipherable gaze.

"Thank you," she managed.

Swallowing, she scooted over and gathered some of the ruffles of her dress to make space for him on the bench.

He took it, folding himself carefully next to her, making no move to touch her as she turned away to wipe her tears and dab at her nose.

"Did he hurt you?" The question was low. Dark. And it made her turn to look at him.

"No, not really. I'm not crying about that."

He nodded before his gaze lowered. "If the violence frightened you, I—"

"*No.*" She put her hand on his arm to stop that thought from forming, and he became instantly rigid beneath her touch. "No, you were wonderful. I don't know what I would have done. What I would have allowed him to do because I was too afraid or embarrassed to stop him."

"Allowed him to do…" Titus didn't finish the thought. He just stared at her hand on his arm as his brows drew together.

"How could *I* have stopped him without ruining everything?" she rushed to explain. "My father would have been furious with me. My reputation ruined. Any chances of a good marriage, to him or otherwise, completely dashed. My—my entire life would have been over. He knew he had put me in that position, I think. That I was truly helpless, because I'd gone with him into the dark. How could I have been so *thoughtless?*" She hit her own knee with the hand that clutched the handkerchief.

A frustrated mélange of emotions welled up inside of her. Resentment. Fear. Animosity. For Michael. For her parents. For the entire dastardly world.

For herself.

"That was—" Her breath hitched on a raw sob. She began to shake with the power of her reaction. "That was my first kiss."

She buried her face into the handkerchief, thinking it felt warm and familiar as she allowed a few more tears to fall. She'd taught herself to cry quietly from early on, and to regain her composure in an instant, forcing it all down beneath a façade of serenity before anyone could ascertain a weakness with which to whip her.

And she might have composed herself now, if a large, gentle hand hadn't splayed on her back and stayed there.

Titus didn't babble meaningless words. Nor did he caress her or crush her to him. He asked no questions and gave no encouragements. He offered comfort merely by being there, by letting her be and allowing her to feel what she needed to feel without the fear of reproof.

It must have been why she curled toward him, tucking her head against his shoulder, breathing in the cedar-sweet smell of his collar and neck. She could think of no other reason to do what was so utterly out of character. Something about the silent strength of him—something she fancied she glimpsed in that alert, opaque gaze of his —drew her toward him like a viper mesmerized by an exotic flute.

His arm cradled her against his side, the other reaching toward her face as he looked down at her with those extraordinary eyes. He'd taken off his gloves, she noted, as his fingers lifted toward her cheek. He hesitated before he touched her, as if waiting for permission.

Nora's lashes swept down, causing more tears to fall as she turned her face into his awaiting palm.

He thumbed away the drops with skin so rough it abraded hers, but still she buried her cheek deeper against his hand, seeking the warmth and strength she found there, tempered by utter gentility and something else she couldn't begin to define.

For the first time in her short life, Nora felt as if the pressure of the entire sky wasn't doing its utmost to crush her into the ground. This boy had strength enough in his shoulders to bear the burden that was *her* for a moment.

And he seemed willing enough.

She couldn't say how long they stayed like that before something restless stirred inside of her. Something that wanted more of him. Of this.

"Titus?" she whispered.

"Yes, Miss Goode?"

"Will you call me Nora? My friends all call me Nora."

46

He paused. "If I took such liberties, I'd lose my position here."

It was odd, him saying that, when they found themselves in such an intimate posture. But, of course. How stupid of her to forget. She wasn't the only one constrained by her station. "I only meant when we're alone."

His breath hitched then, as if something agitated him. "We...should not be alone."

Wanting to soothe him in kind, Nora placed her hand over the one he held to her cheek, the softness of her gloved fingertips snagging over his coarse knuckles.

Beneath her, his shoulder lifted and fell with quickening breaths, and the warmth of his exhales brushed her skin, lightly scented of dessert flavored by port.

The staff wasn't supposed to nip at the food, but she'd always supposed they did, and she was glad he'd had a taste.

He deserved every pleasure.

Suddenly she wanted to know more about him. "How did you know about the Marquess of Blandbury?"

"Doctor Alcott," he said simply.

"You must see him often if you know such intimate things about his patients and swap books from his library."

He shifted a little, as if talking about himself made him uncomfortable. "I work for him four evenings a week and every other Saturday."

"On top of your duties here?"

He nodded.

What a keen mind he must have. She rather appreciated that. "I think it's lovely of you to lend them to Felicity." A smile worked its way through her prior distress, at the thought of her sister's eyes, made unnaturally large by her spectacles, as she stared adoringly up at Titus. "I think she rather fancies you."

He made a sound in his chest that landed somewhere

between amusement and embarrassment, but he made no reply.

She laced her fingers in between his as if she needed to hold onto something in order to make her next confession. "Sometimes I have vague wisps of dreams, or maybe memories, of those days I spent with the fever."

He tensed, and she had the impression that if her hand hadn't held his to her cheek, he would have retracted it.

"I think you were feeding me, singing me lullabies..." Unsure of what was prompting her to behave this way, she turned her face against his skin until her lips grazed the meat of his palm. "Bathing me."

He drew away then, his breath sawing in and out of him with true effort as he turned his back to her. "Don't remember," he rasped.

She couldn't tell if he meant *he* didn't remember, or if he was ordering *her* not to recall. But she *did.* Bits and pieces. She wondered sometimes, how much of it had been real. If he'd taken cooling sponges to her bare skin. If he'd lowered her naked body into baths and then tenderly arranged soft nightgowns over her.

She couldn't help but allow her thoughts to linger on the intimacy of that.

"I didn't ever thank you properly," she said, pressing her hand to his shoulder. "They whisked me off so quickly to that health clinic in Switzerland, and then to finishing school after that. But... I've thought of you often."

So very often.

He said nothing. Did nothing. Just breathed, or at least fought to do so.

Had he thought of her? She wanted to ask. Did she linger in his mind as he did in hers, like the sweet furloughs of the past? A reassuring memory through a miasma of distress and expectation?

"Titus," she breathed, her own heartbeat gaining strength, pressing against her ribs. "Titus, look at me."

His chin touched his shoulder, and she reached out to encourage him to swivel his entire body to face her on the bench.

"I want to thank you," she said, bracketing his tense jaw with both her silk-gloved hands, searching his uniquely handsome face and finding what she hoped for.

Hope and hunger.

"Thank you for *everything*," she whispered. "For then. For tonight. And...for *this*." Following a reckless, unrelenting longing, she pulled his head lower so her lips could press to his.

She found his mouth harder than she'd expected.

Sweeter, too.

They sat like that for a moment, their lips locked and still, as if waiting for the night to catch its breath, because neither of them seemed to be able to.

Then, his mouth became pliant over hers, before he nudged gently forward.

Moving his lips in subtle, whispering sweeps, he took control of the kiss without even seeming to know he'd done it, drugging her with motions that were as languid as they were astonished.

As certain as they were untried.

His hands drew up her arms, but instead of taking liberties, they settled at the band of skin where the hem of her gloves ended above her elbow but below her sleeve. His thumb stroked lightly there, testing the softness, and eliciting more erotic sensation than she'd thought existed.

She'd somehow known it would be like this. That *he* would be like this. Something inside of her had sensed his need, not strictly by the way he looked at her. But in the way he avoided looking.

As if he didn't allow himself to want her.

She was a woman aware of her beauty. One who was

reminded of it by nearly everyone she met. Usually, self-ishly, she wished it were not her defining feature.

Except now.

Because she wanted nothing so much as his desire. The nature of it called to something deep within her. Something as incontrovertible as it was primitive.

And she could do nothing but answer.

When his tongue searched the seam of her lips with a questioning lick, she tentatively opened to him, but not too far. He hovered softly, before venturing into her mouth with the flavor of sweet cream and buttery cake. Not rich like the soufflé they'd had for dessert, but no less delicious.

He didn't stroke or demand, he merely explored and retreated before daring to do it again.

The taste of him ignited an unbearable ache deep within her that, if fed, would become dangerous for them both.

Suddenly Nora was very aware she'd been gone from her own ball for far too long. That she'd be missed, and people would come looking.

Especially since Michael would have returned and, hopefully, been frightened enough by Titus's threat, to make his excuses and leave.

Lord, she wished she could stay here. That she could kiss him all night and all the nights after. Indeed, she couldn't summon the strength to break away.

Seeming to sense this, he reluctantly broke the seal of their mouths, returning to soften the blow with a couple of short, soft tugs with his lips.

She emitted a sigh as he pulled back, thinking he might just be the loveliest being on this earth. A strange and silent creature, as dangerous as he was docile.

"You taste like icing," she murmured. Feeling abruptly shy and ridiculous, she wanted to pluck the words back before they reached him.

"Cake," he explained in that deliberate way of his. "It's my birthday."

"Oh! I had no idea."

"Why would you?"

The words weren't meant to sound like a rebuke, she knew, but she felt it all the same. Why would she know such things about someone so beneath her?

"Well, happy birthday, Titus Conleith," she said, summoning a smile that drew his gaze to her lips. "How old are you now?"

"Seventeen."

Her eyebrows drew up at that. As tall as he'd become, as wise as the soul behind his gaze was, it was easy to forget he remained three years her junior.

"You should get back," he said, echoing her earlier thoughts. Releasing her, he let out a shaky breath, retrieved his gloves, and stood.

Nora felt his absence with a keen sort of ache that almost shamed her. She wasn't a woman of such need. She didn't form attachments, nor did she entertain impossible notions. So...what was this between them?

"I'll go in ahead to make sure that bastard is gone," he offered, pulling the white gloves on to hide the rough fingers he'd only just caressed her with. Ones that would offend any woman in that ballroom.

But not her.

"Of course. Thank you and... Goodnight, Titus."

He gazed down at her a breathless moment, and she almost thought he might reach down, haul her to her feet, and kiss her wits right out of her.

And perhaps more.

Instead he balled his fist at his side and strode away from her, but not before the night breeze carried his words over his shoulder.

"Goodnight... Nora."

Sniffling, Nora looked down at the handkerchief in

her hand and gasped at the initials she found embroidered there.

They were hers.

She'd offered him this very handkerchief years ago in the paddock.

He'd kept it all these years.

*G*oodnight, Nora.

He said it nearly every evening for three blissful months, and it never ceased to vibrate through her with a warm incandescence.

Titus Conleith had been not only her most lovely secret, but also a revelation.

Was it always like this, she wondered, falling in love? It was as if the world—nay—the entire *cosmos* had shifted to make way for the two of them to revel in each other.

And no one seemed to notice.

Or, rather, they'd been too rapt to pay heed to anyone else.

Her father had been not only furious but befuddled by the abject silence emanating from the direction of the Marquess of Blandbury, the man claimed to be inaccessible due to his health. Despite that, or perhaps because of it, the Baron had barely spoken a word to her, presumably moving on to more important matters now that Parliament had resumed session.

Nora still attended balls and soirees, fittings and functions as any dutiful debutante should, but whenever she had a moment to herself, it belonged to Titus, as well.

He'd become the groom she took to assist and accompany on her long, rollicking rides across Rotten Row in Hyde Park. They'd fly over the golden ground of the horse track, their heads low and their hearts racing in time to the hooves of their mounts.

She watched him covertly as they walked the park to cool the animals. How tall and fine he looked astride the bay steed, even among lords more turned out than he.

Titus didn't require a brilliant suit to stand out. To stand above. He did it merely by existing. When he trotted by, men made way for him, and women turned to look at him.

More frequently to gape and admire.

He wore no top hat, as he was no gentleman, though sometimes he'd set a wool cap against the sun or inclement weather. More often, he'd comb his fingers through locks as rich as Spanish chocolate, and they'd settle in the most perfect sweep back from his forehead.

Nora always overheard a dreamy sigh or two added to hers when he thusly contained a mane tousled by a spirited ride.

Extraordinarily, he seemed to be unaware of his effect.

He never flirted with the women who would try to capture his attentions; indeed, he was invariably aloof whilst managing to remain deferential. It was as though he used his politeness to keep people at a distance whilst still retaining their good opinion.

No small skill, that.

His was an honest, uncomplicated confidence. He'd a smooth way of moving about the world in which he existed, with the ease of someone who was born with a certain sense of self-possession. He never asked for anyone's respect or permission because he required neither.

He was who he was. He did what he must, and the rest of the time, he did what he liked.

And dared anyone to stop him. Or maybe he just realized no one would dare try.

There was something so refreshing about that. So unsophisticated and natural.

Nora basked in it. She rolled herself up in his atmosphere like it was a warm blanket, and she wished for nothing more than to stay within the shelter of his blindingly handsome smile for the rest of her days.

He escorted her on picnics, often with Pru or the twins in tow, and they'd all have impassioned discussions. She'd been delighted to discover that beneath all his solemnity he was possessed of a dry humor and a sharp wit that ignited with a quick tinder. He'd regale them about what he learned with Dr. Alcott, and she and Felicity would needle him for the gorier details, most of which he was loath to share. She loved how impassioned and animated he became when he spoke of medicine, his face alight with interest.

She loved that, in him, she had found a genuine companion. A true friend.

But most of all, she looked forward to evenings like this one, where, after his work with Dr. Alcott had finished, he'd scale the trellis to her balcony and slip into her bedroom.

Nora would leave a lantern lit and sit in wait, every hair on her body vibrating with anticipation. She'd brush out her curls until they glimmered, and smooth her skin with cream, touching a tiny bit of rose water behind her ears.

And when he would pause in the door like he did now, as if he needed a moment of stillness to take in the sight of her, she positively thrummed with feminine delight.

He didn't need to tell her she was beautiful; she could see it in the way those golden eyes ignited with a molten flame before he came to her. Before his hands sifted through the waves of her hair, setting every nerve of her body alight with sensation.

Though he'd fiercely protected her virtue, even from

himself, he was all wickedness when he touched her like this.

When their lips met, she forgot that her feelings for him were forbidden.

When his hands skimmed across her skin, the coarse fibers of his fingertips snagging on the softness of her, she allowed herself a small sense of wonder. A tiny ember of hope.

She lost herself in the discovery of the peaks and planes of his topography. And she found herself in the reflection of worship with which he touched her.

Each night he came to her unlocked a new depth of passion. At first, it'd been chaste kisses and broad smiles. Then the kisses had become wilder, the caresses bolder.

More intimate.

Her nightdress began to disappear, and so did his trousers.

She learned the shape of his need. He learned the depths of her desire. And together, with breathless astonishment, they'd discovered the pleasure of which the human body was capable.

Tonight was different, though. Something more primitive lurked beneath his caress. A base and carnal urgency that called to everything that made her a woman.

He was no longer learning. *He knew.*

He no longer sought. *He claimed.*

Nora found herself beneath him, felt her legs open so he might settle between as she stretched with a liquid, boneless languor brought on by thorough attentions.

His movements and kisses had been so entirely masculine. Fervent. Arduous.

Possessive.

This new dynamic from him had excited her with such ferocity it had almost frightened her.

Because she wanted to claim him as well.

She wanted ownership of the heart that, even now, felt

as though it were locked away in some hollow place. Sometimes, when he seemed very far away, she wanted to rip him open and lay him bare. If only to understand what constantly remained out of her reach.

Was this love? This desperate, wanton need? This endless curiosity?

This relentless infatuation?

As he hovered above her, this man who was barely not a boy, she smoothed a dark forelock away from his face, and smiled as it fell right back in place.

His arms trembled. His eyes burned with need. With the question. With a flame that matched the one burning in her heart.

She wrapped her body around him, welcoming him in.

Not a word was said in the darkness, as their virtue was relinquished to the other. They communicated in sighs and hitches of breath. They spoke with their fingertips and their features, the language that was created the moment one human had ever desired another. And though there was a flash of pain, there was pleasure, too.

And Nora knew he would forever own her body, heart, and soul.

THE NEXT MORNING

*N*ora decided to forgo a ride in Hyde Park, as she twinged and ached in secret places. The need to see Titus was overwhelming today; not only did her physical body feel a bit raw, but so did her soul. His quiet eyes would soothe her as they always did. His voice would lend her the reassurance she needed. It was silly, she knew, this desire to be certain that now that he'd had her body, his heart was still true.

She tried to find him in the stables, if only to tell him not to bother saddling her horse and to suggest a stroll, instead, to somewhere neither of them would be recognized.

They might even walk arm in arm like a true couple and discuss things that were not so idle. Like their dreams for the future.

Finding the stables empty of all but the horses, she mounted the narrow steps to his room above the mews, overlooking the hubbub of the street. Often, she would find him there poring over a medical text, and she'd have to distract him with soft kisses to his neck before convincing him to do something frivolous with her.

She knocked on his door before depressing the latch.

"Titus? You're not still sleeping, are you? I thought we might—"

"Honoria."

That one word pinned her boots to the shabby wood floor as her father stood like a titan in the middle of the room, advertising just how small and sparce it truly was.

Glacial blue eyes speared her with such abject condemnation, her legs threatened to give way.

"So it's true," he spat, reading the guilt that must have splashed across her face with a fiery crimson hue. "Really, Honoria, your behavior is beyond the pale."

"Where is he?" she gasped, taking in the empty cot and the one scarred trunk now open and devoid of all personal effects.

"He's been thrown onto the streets like the rubbish he is." His boots made such a terrible thunder against the rickety wooden loft floor as he moved to the window to survey Mayfair, as if to make certain Titus was not still out there.

Nora's heart did a swan dive into her stomach as tears pricked her eyes. He was already gone? She knew that she stood on the precipice of a life-altering cataclysm, and she did her best to rein in her thoughts, which bucked and galloped like a panicked horse. Now was not the time to be irrational or overwrought. Clarence Goode did not react well to emotion or sentiment. He needed her to be logical. Amiable. Measured. Disciplined.

She took a deep breath. "Allow me to explain what is—"

"There is only one plausible explanation when a boy is climbing down from your balcony in the wee hours of the morning," he said with a lethal calm, though his jowls trembled with a barely leashed anger. "A *son* dallying with the help is understandable, I've done it myself from time to time, but you *know* better!"

He whirled away from the window to stab an accusatory finger at her. "A woman's worth is her virtue, as it says in the Good Book. And I don't care to know how far you've carried on with this boy, but you've shamed me, Honoria, and you've disgraced yourself. I can barely stand to look at you."

She swallowed the disgust his words brought forth in her, and squared her chin against him. "I have not dallied with Titus, Father, I truly care for him. I-I love him. He's honest and kind and he's endlessly good. He saved my life."

"That doesn't mean he gets to help himself to your body! I'd rather you had succumbed to fever than to a coal boy."

She stepped forward, clasping her hands together in front of her wounded heart. "You don't mean that."

"Don't I?" he fumed.

"Titus has done much more for our family and our household than shoveling coal. He is going to be a doctor, like Alcott, who you consider your friend and social equal. He can make a good living. He could be part of our family."

He slammed the lid of the trunk closed hard enough to splinter it, causing her to jump. "Wake. Up. You stupid girl. Alcott is the fifth son of a very fortunate Viscount. Considering a street urchin like yours would ruin us all. Would you do that to your sisters? Would you soil Pru's chances at happiness? I'll have a hard enough time offloading the twins, what with Mercy's relentless mouth and Felicity's ridiculous mind. *You* will love whom I tell you to love, and that's the end of it!"

"I will not!" Though lanced with guilt at the thought of her sisters surviving a scandal she'd created, she likewise shook with temper and fear, longing and loss. She'd never stood up to her father before. To anyone really. She'd been born biddable, but *this* she could not abide. "I'm of age, Father, I'll leave with him. We'll go far away and we'll make it on our own. You'll never have to see me again. No one ever need know what I've done. You can make up whatever fiction you wish. Tell people I'm dead if that helps the situation."

He stunned her by throwing his head back and barking out a harsh and mirthless laugh, before striding to her and grasping her by the arm. "If you do anything of the sort, I'll ruin that boy until he *wishes* he were dead. Do you hear me?" He shook her for emphasis, and she let out a gasp of pain as his fingers bit into her arm. "I'll make certain he can find no work in this city. *Worse.* I'll have him thrown into Newgate for molesting you. I have friends in the police and on the Queen's Bench. You know what happens to lads handsome as he is, in prison?"

Her eyes widened. "You wouldn't."

"Furthermore, I'll send you to Bedlam for being a disobedient wretch. They'll shave off your pretty hair and electrocute you into submission. Is that what you want?" He stood over her like a wrathful god, eyes flashing with condemnation. His hair and beard, once handsomely fair, now threaded with shocks of silver, added to the effect.

A terror Nora had never known gripped her. This was her father, a man known to be as extravagant as he was insouciant. Certainly, he'd never been a warm parent, but she'd not thought him capable of such dire, horrid cruelty.

"Answer carefully, Honoria," he spat. "Your next words will determine both of your futures. I can make certain that loving you will be the worst thing that ever happened to that boy."

She had to swallow over a lump of fear cutting off her available supply of air. "What—what do you want me to do?"

"I want you to never see him again. And I want you out of this house so I don't have to be reminded of your ungrateful wretchedness daily."

That was a blessing, she thought. She couldn't wait to leave.

"You'll marry William Mosby, Viscount Woodhaven, at the month's end. I'll post the bans this morning."

"Woodhaven?" Her breath hitched on the word as she shrank from him.

"Yes, the Cresthaven and Woodhaven titles were created by Richard III some four hundred years ago. Our families fought for the Yorks together. We're distant cousins. This would be an excellent match, under the circumstances."

Nora had danced with William Mosby at a function some months ago. There'd been a neediness in their interaction she didn't at all like. A strange sense of possession. Something frenetic and frankly, sinister.

"I'll have to rely on Pru's sweet nature and secondary beauty to secure someone higher than an Earl," he groused as if to himself.

"But, *Papa*," she pleaded.

"I won't hear it." He released her with a rough shove toward the door. "Get out of my sight. The next time I lay eyes on you will be at your wedding."

HONORIA DIDN'T SLEEP FOR DAYS. SHE SAT ON THE EDGE OF her bed, staring at her balcony door, knowing beyond the shadow of a doubt that Titus would find a way to her.

On the fourth night, the latch clicked at one in the morning, revealing a Titus who looked as haunted and haggard as she felt.

It took every ounce of her self-possession not to fling herself into his arms.

"Nora," he breathed as he tumbled into her room, reaching for her. "Nora, are you all right?"

She stood and shoved his hands away from her,

turning her back to him so she didn't have to look. "You need to go, Titus. You need to *go* and not ever darken my door again."

"No. Don't speak like that." His fingers gripped her arms and pulled her shoulder blades against his solid chest as he buried his cheek into her hair.

She wanted nothing so much as to turn into his embrace, which was why she kept her back as straight as steel, her every muscle coiled with tension.

Lord, but she was cold. It felt as though ice ran through her veins rather than blood.

How could she do this?

"Come away with me, Nora," he implored, his hand cupping at her cheek and nudging to turn her toward him. "I know you're frightened, but we can be together."

"I don't see how," she mourned, soaking in his touch, in the hope his voice conveyed. Hope she was about to shatter.

"I've secured a position in Doctor Alcott's service," he told her urgently. "Next year I'm taking the medical exams. I've rooms to stay in and a steady income. We've a future, Nora. Just pack a case and we'll leave now."

"How could you even consider a future like that would appeal to me?" she bit out, her pain at least grating through her throat to lend her voice a harsh rasp that could have been convincing as cruelty.

His fingers tightened, and she was glad she didn't have to face him just yet, as she could feel him resist the astonished implication that it might not just be her father that would keep them apart.

"What are you saying?" he asked carefully.

"You think I want to live in a dingy room over Doctor Alcott's surgery?" she asked, summoning all the starched, imperious snobbery her upbringing had imparted to her. "You want me to malinger there while you earn pennies and ignore me for your studies? You want me to raise babies and scrub floors and cook your dinner whilst you toil away?"

She would have done it. Anything to be freed of this gilded prison. Of the walls that closed in nightly and the cage of her parents' strictures and expectations.

She would have done anything but destroy him.

His hands fell away from her and the lack of warmth against her skin stung like the most unrelenting winter's wind. "I—I know it's not what you were raised to want."

God, she could feel him searching, could sense the frantic scrambles of his thoughts as he tried to catch up with a situation that was unraveling in a way he never expected. She wanted to hold him. To tell him what was in her heart. In her soul. To make him understand what they were both up against.

But she knew him. Knew he would fight for her because he was so noble. So true.

He was the man she wanted. A future with him was exactly what she desired.

"You wouldn't have to serve me, Nora," he said gently. "I would keep you fed. I would keep you happy. If you'd just give me a little time, I'd find a way to keep some semblance of the life you—"

"Stop!" She whirled on him, hiding her sob with a slap to his cheek. "You don't get to keep me at all."

The expression in his eyes pierced her with more pain than any she could inflict on him. The sheer bewilderment laced with betrayal. The pain.

And then, the hardening of his features as he began to believe...

He'd never know. He'd never understand what this took from her. She might be stomping on his heart, but she was rending her very soul from her skin and casting it into the abyss. She was killing herself in slow increments, knowing that the years ahead would be nothing but torture. That she would be the shell of a woman, haunting a body that no longer belonged to her.

Because her heart would be wherever he was.

"It was me who had you sacked," she lied. "Our dalliance was a bit of fun, to be sure, but I always credited you with enough sense to know nothing would come of it. And when we were found out due to your recklessness, it became more of a bother than it was a diversion. And so, I think it best we end things here."

To her astonishment, he didn't give up. "Nora, this isn't you! Tell me what's happened."

"I'm getting married."

Her words had more effect on him than her physical slap. He flinched, then froze, his body becoming unnaturally still.

"That's right." She notched her chin up higher. "I'm going to be a Viscountess, a small comfort, seeing as how you lost me a Marquess."

His expression became thunderous. "You were glad when I stopped that—"

"Was I?" She shrugged. "Perhaps I didn't feel ready then, to be a wife. But now..." Her gaze fell upon the bed where they'd made the sweetest love, so enraptured with each other it was easy to believe that no one else in the world existed. That they could overcome anything.

What fools they'd been.

And now they'd pay for it. She'd pay the most dearly.

His sharp intake of breath told her that her dagger had met its mark. That her sharp words had sawed through the invisible chord that seemed to link them together no matter where in the world they stood. All she had to do was make certain the link was severed forever.

That she smothered all hope.

"Don't make a fool of yourself by doing something so pathetic as begging, Titus," she said with all the frost threatening to harden her from the inside out. She was surprised she couldn't see her breath as she uttered the cruel words she'd learned from her father. "I can no longer stand the sight of you."

He stood looking at her as if she'd shot him, his features a mélange of denial and rage, before they, too, smoothed out into the cool lake of unrippled inscrutability she was used to.

"Goodnight, Nora," he said crisply before he strode to her door.

As she watched him go, she remembered wondering before if that sparkling, incandescent obsession, that cocoon of bliss and warmth in which they'd been ensconced, had been what true love felt like.

And here was her answer.

No.

This was love.

Sacrifice. Regret. Pain.

Love, the purest love, was diving into the lake of brimstone and hellfire, and drowning in it willingly, if only to gain freedom for the one who owned your heart.

Titus would have the opportunity to go to medical college. He'd heal people and find fulfillment and satisfaction in the worthy life he built, free of a powerful enemy like her father. He'd—no doubt—find a girl who loved him and could provide him with fat, cooing babies and happy chaos.

The idea stole her breath, it was so painful.

This was love.

And she was one raw, bleeding wound he could never heal.

A SAWBONES IN SOUTHWARK

London, 1880

"*I*f you don't hold still, I'm going to have to restrain you," Dr. Titus Conleith warned.

"Sorry, guv," said Mr. Ludlow, the dock worker currently perched on his table, gesticulating wildly for a man with sutures only half stitched. "But I just never seen any'fing like it, 'ave I? Sir Carlton Morley, the *bloody* Chief Inspector of Scotland *bloody* Yard, crawling about on a Southwark warehouse roof. Like a fucking spider he was, shooting his rifle into the windows. Glass shattered everywhere, and as I looks up, one sticks me right in me bloody 'ead."

"Morley, did this, you say?" he asked. "Here in Southwark?"

"As I live and breathe," Ludlow vowed.

Titus had met Carlton Morley when they served together in the second Anglo-Afghan war. He'd picked a bullet from the Chief Inspector's thigh once upon a time, and in the years since, they'd shared a bachelor's meal out at their club now and again.

They sometimes reminisced over how they had lost

Kandahar and what a blood-soaked ordeal it had been. Then they'd taken Kabul, which had been even worse.

Often in the throes of haunted insobriety, they'd share a hackney to their respective homes and part, only to do it again the next time their schedules permitted.

An unceasingly decent bloke was Morley.

These days, Titus avoided the chief inspector as the man had recently married none other than Prudence Goode under rather scandalous circumstances.

For such a large city, London was certainly a small world.

It brought Titus no little amount of pleasure that the Baron of Cresthaven's second daughter went to a man like Morley, who had been raised in a Whitechapel gutter.

He'd someday have to get the story from the horse's mouth, when he could trust himself to sit across from his old friend and keep from inquiring about—

As he always did, Titus firmly redirected his thoughts away from Morley's new sister-in-law.

Nora.

"What I would have given to stay," the man sighed, leaning in conspiratorially. "As Dorian Blackwell, his *own self*, showed up just as I was being drug 'ere by me mate, Stodgy Tim. It seemed to me like he and Morley 'us after the same poor ponce in the warehouse."

"You don't say." Titus tugged the suture clamps tight to make certain that if Ludlow moved again, they'd make him uncomfortable. He absorbed himself with stitching the wound so as not to reveal the odd amalgamation of tensions swirling within him.

The Chief Inspector of Scotland Yard and the king of the London underworld after the same enemy? There were certain to be casualties. He knew Morley from the army. He knew Blackwell from the streets.

How they knew each other was anyone's guess.

By right of their professions, alone, they were natural adversaries.

Titus worried for Prudence. A fondness for all four of the Goode girls had developed during his tenure at Cresthaven. He truly hoped that Pru—a child he remembered as sweet and mischievous—was unharmed. That Ludlow had the story completely wrong.

Was a war between the police and the underworld here at his doorstep?

The very thought curdled his stomach. How the streets would run red with blood if Blackwell and Morley truly went to battle. There weren't enough surgeons in the Empire to clean up after such a nightmare.

Titus exchanged a meaningful glance with his nurse, a battleax in her thirties by the name of Euphemia Higgins. Effie's hands were almost as large as his, and twice as gentle. She could just as easily carry a two-hundred-pound man as she could swaddle a newborn, and he'd follow her level head into a battle before most officers he'd served with. Beneath her nurse's cap and frizzy blond hair, was a brain with enviable computation capabilities. Were *she* the one with a medical degree from Cambridge, she'd rule the world and then some.

"So, you're not certain if anyone else was wounded?" he asked Mr. Ludlow with increasing urgency.

Any chance at a reply was squelched by a commotion outside.

Most people who called at Titus Conleith's Southwark Surgery door also lurked on death's doorstep. Therefore, patients or their loved ones rarely knocked politely. They pounded and screamed. Begged for help. Sometimes, they begged for death. He'd treated people who bled or leaked from every possible orifice, starting at the eyes and concluding at the other end.

Having his door splintered at the hinges with one kick, however, was entirely new.

A good surgeon trained himself not to startle. Titus had been educated with explosions rocking the earth beneath him, and bullets whizzing past his ears, so he was—luckily for Mr. Ludlow—more imperturbable than most.

"The door was unlocked," he blithely reproached Dorian Blackwell, the Black Heart of Ben More, whose boots thundered like the devil's on the rickety old floors of the clinic.

Doors didn't close to a man like him.

Not even Newgate could hold Blackwell, or so the story went. His suit, hair, and one eye were as dark as his heart, the other eye covered by a patch that almost hid the evidence of a vicious slash from his brow to his nose. The scar made his grim expression sinister as he surveyed the surgery with a critical frown.

"Someone's been shot, Conleith. Which table?"

Titus relinquished Ludlow's final sutures to Nurse Higgins, before marching past the one other empty examination table to pull back the curtains of the clinic's makeshift operation room. He'd done everything from delivering babies to removing ruptured spleens and appendixes here. Though, he usually dug bullets out of criminals after dark, and it was barely five in the evening.

"Tell me Morley's not on your heels, Blackwell," he demanded, glad to be one of the few men in the world tall enough to glare *down* at the Black Heart of Ben More as he marched past him to the sink to ruthlessly scrub his hands. "If there's a clash between the law and the underworld in my surgery, then you can find someone *else* to stitch up your army of reprobates and degenerates in the middle of the night; do I make myself clear?"

Blackwell, who had killed men for lesser offenses, merely held up his hands in a gesture of good will. "I forgot how fast news travels in these parts. I imagine Morley will be along shortly, but not for the reason you fear."

"Oh? Enlighten me." Nearly finished stripping the skin from his hands, Titus moved up his wrist and forearms with the stringent suds.

More footsteps clomped up the few stairs from the street into his surgery, these weighted down by the burden of a stretcher. As he stood at the sink, Titus's back was to the door, and Blackwell's bulky shoulders blocked any view he might have had.

"Where do we put her?" a rough voice inquired.

Her?

Titus froze, his hand at his elbow, his breath caught in his throat.

"Operating table at the back," Higgins directed in her starched Cockney accent.

"Is—is it Pru—Morley's wife?" he asked, after clearing dread out of his throat.

"No, Prudence is unharmed. She was kidnapped by her own brother-in-law, who used her as a hostage to not only escape the police, but some rather ruthless cocaine smugglers, even by my standards." Blackwell examined him oddly as Titus rinsed his hands. "The villain shot his own wife before Morley eviscerated him with frankly astonishing rifleman skills."

Nurse Higgins—the marvelous creature—had finished Ludlow's stitches in record time and left Mr. Ludlow to bandage his own wound so she could scrub her hands and retrieve the sterilized surgical instruments from the carbolic acid.

Suddenly Titus didn't want to turn to look. Not because he was bothered by blood…

But because he'd finally processed the information Blackwell had just imparted.

Prudence Morley—originally Prudence Goode—only had one brother-in-law. William Mosby, the Viscount Woodhaven, who'd just shot his own wife before falling victim to Morley's rifle.

His own wife.

The room tilted as Titus turned to find his worst nightmare on his operating table.

Nora.

FROM THE VEIN

*T*itus's hands had never been so unsteady during a procedure.

Never had he barked orders so terribly at Higgins as he sheared Nora's blood-soaked gown from her alarmingly pale, unconscious body. Nor had he growled commands so fiercely at a man as dangerous as Blackwell, to wash his hands and prepare to help.

Never had he prayed to every saint his father had believed in with such dire fervency as when he searched for an exit wound. Nor given such thanks when he found one.

The bullet had gone through her, but the sheer amount of blood pouring from her shoulder meant the situation was increasingly dire.

"Her pulse and breaths are thready," Higgins informed him, timing them with her watch. "I shouldn't like to use the anesthesia."

"Nor I, but this amount of blood tells me an axillary vein may have been nicked, and if I get in there to repair it and she moves in the slightest…"

He couldn't say it. He couldn't even consider the prospect that the only woman he ever loved and hated would bleed to death on his own table.

73

By his own hand.

For the first time in his career, Titus's choices were truly untenable. Like most doctors, he'd learned to accept early on that his profession was merely a way to delay death, not to defeat it.

But, regardless of what Alcott had taught him at such an early age, *she* could never be just a dying body.

Because death wasn't an option.

"I'll meticulously count every breath, Doctor," Higgins said in a gentle manner he'd never heard her use before, as she placed the anesthesia mask over Nora's mouth and nose. "She'll get through this."

Nora. Nora. Her name became the rhythm of his heartbeat as he delved into the intricate sinew of her shoulder. He had to irrigate away alarming amounts of blood to find the correct vein, and then to clamp and stitch it.

Fate aligned with his expertise, as every surgeon knew that each body was made up of similar constructions that could also be as vast and varied in their particular assembly as stars in the sky. Miraculous good fortune deemed that the vein was easily found and that the nick was small, or she'd have expired before they could have loaded her in the carriage.

Titus didn't breathe as he released the clamp, until he saw that he'd repaired the damage.

His relief was such that her name escaped him on a whisper, and he fought to keep the starch in his knees.

Nora.

He wasn't aware he'd been sweating until Higgins passed a cloth over his forehead and upper lip, firmly planting him into the present.

No, he reminded himself. Not *Nora*. Not to him.

Lady Honoria Mosby, Viscountess Woodhaven.

Now that the vein had been repaired, he still had to work on the other tissue and sinew surrounding the wound.

A tremor coursed through him as he looked down at her torso, bare but for where a strip of cloth placed by Higgins covered her breasts. *God*, she'd always been a small and fragile creature, but now her bones seemed like that of a sparrow's. The years hollowed out her cheeks, and dark shadows smudged beneath her eyes. Her features were still magnificent, though, and razor sharp. Her lashes black fans against porcelain skin made ashen from the loss of blood.

She was still the most beautiful woman he'd ever laid his eyes upon.

Still.

Always.

Which was why he'd resolved long ago to never fucking lay eyes upon her again.

But here they were.

In the stormy chaos of life, Titus prided himself on being a smooth lake of glass. Reflective and serene.

But right now, his thoughts spun like a tornado, flinging debris at him that he couldn't seem to avoid.

"Distract me, Blackwell," he ordered as he handed the man the clamp to discard, and selected other instruments.

The Black Heart of Ben More—who had assisted in a few late-night surgeries for lack of a nurse—had returned from the sink where he'd removed his coat, rolled up his shirtsleeves, and scrubbed his own hands. He looked at Titus askance. "I rather assumed you'd need to focus."

"It's difficult to explain, but often distraction helps me to concentrate." Titus bent over her, triple-checking his work on her vein before stitching the other sinew. He wished like hell her color wasn't so grey and her breath wasn't so shallow. That he didn't suddenly feel like that helpless boy of fourteen scrambling to save her precious life for the first time. "Since my other nurse, Miss Michaels, isn't here to assist nor read to me, that responsibility falls to you."

"You wish me to...read to you?"

"No, dammit, just—talk to me. I don't know. Tell me what the devil happened."

Blackwell looked as if he might argue, but something in Titus's countenance must have convinced him because he sighed and relented. "It's a rather sordid tale, but from what I gather, her husband was—if you'll pardon my technical language, Higgins—a fucking lunatic."

Higgins, a woman used to every curse word in the Queen's English, asked, "Why shoot his own wife, the poor lamb?"

"On a bit of a killing spree, her husband was," Dorian said with a grim sarcasm. "Do you remember the Earl of Sutherland, the one who Prudence was supposed to marry before she supposedly murdered him?"

Titus gave a curt nod. "I remember reading that in the papers...didn't believe it for a moment."

"Well, come to find out, Woodhaven killed Sutherland and a handful of other men who were reportedly Stags of St. James."

Titus wondered at Nurse Higgins's astonished gasp until she clarified. "You mean... the male prostitutes?" She whispered the last word, appropriately scandalized.

"Just so." Blackwell nodded.

"Was he...were they lovers of his?"

"Apparently not," Dorian answered blithely. "It was a revenge killing, you see. Woodhaven systematically murdered anyone who shared his wife's bed."

Titus dropped his suture clamps with an embarrassingly loud clatter, effectively putting a stop to all conversation. He took a precious breath to compose himself before directing Blackwell where to find another sterile instrument.

He didn't make mistakes like this. He *couldn't*. Not when the stakes were so high.

Nora had taken her husband's best friend to her bed? She'd paid men—a *handful* of men—for sex?

How the years had changed her. Or perhaps they hadn't...

She'd been a stranger to him the night she'd sent him away; perhaps that was when she'd truly been revealed to him.

Clean clamps appeared in his hand, and he immediately went back to work, muttering to Blackwell out of the side of his mouth. "If you ever tire of a life of crime, you'd have an excellent career as a nurse ahead of you."

Blackwell's chortle was nearly mirthless. "Well now, I'm almost completely legitimate these days. I've an angel of a wife and two cherubic miscreants with my name. One might even call me respectable."

"If you find me that one, I'll find you a liar," Titus jested, grateful to the man for helping to release some of the tension.

Higgins, however, had to satisfy her bottomless curiosity. "If her husband was a murderer, then, what's this I heard about cocaine?"

"Apparently, Woodhaven was using his father-in-law's shipping company to smuggle the drug into the city, and some corrupt police officers to deal to the public," Blackwell answered.

Titus's brow crimped as he tried to work out the angle of a lunatic. "Why smuggle? It's not as if cocaine is illegal. Many of my associates use it as medicine."

From beside him, Blackwell made a derisive sound. "And you don't?"

Titus shook his head, then steadied himself over a more complicated stitch. "I don't like the side effects. Nor the addictive properties. There are more effective treatments that have been more thoroughly studied."

"I approve," Blackwell announced. "I predict that, like opium, more ill will come of it than good. However, it is addictive, inexpensive, and abundant on the black market. Men are making fortunes."

"Did Woodhaven?"

Titus had the sense that Dorian shrugged, but he couldn't look over just now to check.

"I believe he was beginning to, though no one knows how deep his cocaine smuggling reaches, and he'll never tell, seeing as how they're scraping his teeth off the wall of the warehouse where Morley's bullet planted them."

Titus dared a glance at Nora's face, glad it was currently covered by the anesthesia mask. "Do they suspect she had anything to do with it?"

Blackwell hesitated. "That I don't know. Whatever she's done, she was bloody brave, trading her life for her sister's at the warehouse."

Suddenly, it occurred to Titus to ask about the Black Heart of Ben More's involvement in all this. "Was he smuggling for you?"

Blackwell's incensed gasp was too overdone to be serious. "He was smuggling for the Fauves, I'll have you know. Something of a rival, once upon a time."

"The Fauves?" Titus searched his extremely limited French vocabulary. "Beasts?"

"Wild beasts, technically." He felt more than watched Blackwell roll his eyes. "Fucking smugglers with delusions of grandeur."

"Did they ever have children?" Titus didn't know the question was about to leave his lips until it materialized.

"How should I know? I don't socialize with Fauves."

"No, I mean she and Woodhaven."

"Evidently not," Blackwell said with no small amount of pity. "With no heir, she effectively has nothing. Perhaps a stipend, if her father is kind."

He knew that bastard was anything but kind.

Not wanting to hear any more, Titus worked in silence for a while as he looked down at her, wondering what tomorrow would bring in either of their lives.

He could feel Dorian's eyes on him with a niggling prickle long before the man spoke. "Before she lost consciousness, she acted like she knew you. She—*begged* us to bring her here. Demanded it."

God. He didn't want to know that. He didn't want to feel the extra beats that information threaded into his heart.

"I—worked in the Goode household as a lad," he said by way of explanation.

"Did you know her well?" Blackwell ventured.

The question caused an explosion of rage and wrath to tumble through his chest. He wasn't *this* man. He didn't have *these* feelings. He'd ruthlessly stuffed any sort of sentiment he had for her down into the deepest recesses of that clear, glass lake. Somewhere in the reeds and the shadows that no one could dredge up. That was where she lived. He'd never even looked twice at a dark-haired woman.

In fact, his current lover was a buxom girl with generous breasts, copper-gold hair, and a giving mouth.

Nora—Lady Woodhaven.

She was ancient history. And yet something stirred within him. An echo of intensity he'd suffered on her behalf as a boy. Did he know her well? He'd thought so.

And then she'd proven him wrong.

Blackwell inspected his work with an appreciative sound. "Did she mean something to you?" he prodded.

Titus speared him with a look so sharp, it could have drawn blood.

Blackwell's brow arched. "Say no more."

IN THE LIGHT OF DAY

P   *lease don't hate me.*
    Nora had made the silent appeal so many times in the past couple of days, it'd become a prayer. A chant. Both an invocation and a benediction.

At first, she'd not said it out loud because she was incapable of speech. A miasma of agonies occasionally intercepted by a sweet, dreamy numbness, had taken days from her. She'd swam in a lake of her own shame and sorrow, drowning in the dark of her unconscious, plagued by dreams and memories of blood and cruelty and fear.

She'd surface from the dark to a world of white. White-hot pain lanced through her chest and arm, whilst blinding-white fluttering veils obscured the world from view.

Then, Titus would appear—a miracle haloed by all that purity—frowning down at her from features older and more brutal than she remembered. She would drink in the sight of him like a condemned soul would their last glance of salvation, fingers twitching with the need to smooth that frown from his dignified brow.

She knew her limbs were incapable; to move would

only cause her pain, so she'd simply gaze at him and try to remember how her dry, swollen tongue worked.

In these brief moments of semi-lucidity, she would catalogue the changes wrought in this Titus from the one who resided in her precious memory.

His hair had darkened to a rich umber, though that unruly forelock still wanted to rest above his eye. The crests of his cheeks stood out in stark relief from features once angled by youth and now squared by maturity. His eyes, though etched with a few more lines than before, were still the color of brilliant sunlight through a glass of young whiskey. Light enough to glimmer golden against skin kissed by a foreign sun.

His lips moved, and the rumble of his voice would transfix her so utterly, the words fluttered in her mouth like a riot of butterflies disturbed by a predator.

Don't hate me.

She'd try so hard to say it, until a prick in her arm would drag her away from him. Back to that place where vivid dreams would first seduce her, then lash at her as they turned into nightmares.

Sometimes when she surfaced, other dear faces would hover above her in the white. Prudence, her features like a younger, fuller mirror of her own, the space between her eyebrows a furrow of worry. She spoke of forgiveness and love, and wiped away the tears that leaked from Nora's eyes into her hair.

Felicity's emotion would fog her spectacles, so she'd keep her thoughts to herself, deciding instead to read aloud, her gentle voice a soothing melody in the chaos of Nora's unruly dreams.

Mercy would often take her hand, squeezing too tightly as she bade her—commanded her—to recover. To win whatever battle she must in order to return to them.

Sometimes a stern-looking woman with a corona of fair, disobedient hair would startle her awake, only to pacify her with unexpected gentility whilst she took care of necessities.

In those moments, Nora would become certain that she'd merely dreamed Titus and her beloved sisters into existence, and she was really trapped in some strange sort of purgatory, awaiting her sentencing to hell.

Just as she began to despair that the floating void would keep her forever, Titus's voice breached the haze with a new clarity as he held a genial conversation in her periphery.

When Nora surfaced, she was both delighted and dismayed to discover that she was herself. Her vision swam, her body was unnaturally heavy, and her shoulder throbbed like the very devil, but not so urgently as her disquiet heart.

She wasn't dead. William hadn't killed her.

Would wonders never cease?

Information permeated her muddled senses incrementally as she took in her surroundings. The white sheets acted as some sort of privacy partition in what she assumed was a hospital. Her nose twitched at scents unfamiliar to any hospital she'd ever visited. Something stringent and clean permeated the distinctive aroma of creosote and coal, horses, petrol, and the brine and grime of the river, all amalgamating into an atmosphere of industry.

Turning her head, she caught her breath as either the early-morning or late-afternoon sun—she couldn't be certain which—cast perfect shadows of people on the other side of the sheet.

She watched the pantomime with arrested interest.

An astonishingly tall, wide-shouldered man braced his knee against the table where another man lay. With a strong, brutal motion, he gave the patient's arm a mighty wrench.

Nora heard the shoulder go into the socket before the patient's bark of pain tugged at her heart.

A smile also tugged at the corner of her lips as she listened to a sonorous baritone soothe and encourage as the tall man made a sling and secured his patient's arm to his chest.

Years at Cambridge still never trained the Yorkshire out of Titus's voice. His vowels were as long and lush as ever.

Nora knew she had any great number of things to be agonizing over. Her life had fragmented in one catastrophic explosion, and she lay in the crater with the damage yet to be entirely assessed.

And yet, even though the pain in her shoulder became increasingly insistent, she allowed herself the sweet gift of this unguarded moment to listen to a voice she'd never expected to hear again.

Titus Conleith.

His manner was everything she remembered, both aloof and kind. But there was a gruffness to his tone that she didn't recognize, as if fatigue had paved his throat with gravel and pitch.

After finishing with his patient, his shadow drew closer, and Nora couldn't say why she feigned sleep before he approached.

Perhaps she wasn't ready to learn what he thought of her after all these years.

He paused at her bedside for a moment too long, and she simply listened to the breath he drew into his lungs and exhaled over her.

They were once again sharing the same air. She could hardly believe it.

In response, her breaths became shorter, less constant, catching as he reached down and pulled the bedclothes away from her shoulders.

Strange, that this should be happening again. That

he'd brought her back from the edge of death a second time.

Had he bathed her as he had when they were younger? Did he care to?

She clenched her jaw against the pain as he ever so gently checked beneath the clean bandage that the astonishingly strong nurse had applied a few hours ago.

Her eyes cracked open of their own accord, hungry for the sight of him.

Nora had always known he'd make an even more handsome man than he'd been a lad, but she'd never guessed he'd grow even taller than he'd been at seventeen. His wide jaw and sharp chin were buttressed by a perfectly starched collar. The cream of his shirt made brilliant by a bronze vest that looked exquisitely tailored to his deep chest and long torso.

In contrast, he wore no jacket, his tie was charmingly askew, and his cheeks wanted shaving. His shadow beard was tinted more russet than dark, advertising his Irish roots.

He didn't notice her assessment of him as his gaze inspected her wound with absorbed thoroughness.

Evidently gratified by what he found, he replaced the bandage and, with utmost care, tugged the hospital gown back into place. Lingering, he pulled the bedclothes to cover her and smoothed the edge over her good arm with a large palm, as if unable to abide a wrinkle.

It was the first time anyone had touched her with deference in as long as she could remember.

"Titus." His name escaped as a rasp from a throat dry with disuse and tight with emotion.

He straightened, yanking his hand away as if she'd burned him.

Their gazes met for a moment so fraught with intensity, it would have struck her down had she not already been prone. Every word ever said and unsaid between them overflowed the filmy white chamber with a tension so thick she could have plucked entire expletives out of thin air.

In the space of a blink, all expression evaporated from his face, and a shutter made of iron slammed down behind his eyes.

"Doctor Conleith," he corrected with careful dispassion.

With those two words, he drew the boundaries between the continents separating them, and erected fortifications that would have protected against an entire fleet of Viking invaders.

It was what she deserved, but it still devastated her.

Don't hate me. Please.

She opened her mouth, unable to truly believe they had a moment alone.

"Higgins, it seems Lady Woodhaven is awake," he clipped, effectively cutting her off.

"Is she now?" The sturdy nurse appeared at the head of her bed as if quite by magic, and leaned over to press a hand to her brow before taking a lantern from the side of her bed to shine in her eyes. Both doctor and nurse bent to check in each eye with an almost comical thoroughness.

For what, Nora couldn't begin to guess.

"Welcome back to the land of the living, Lady Woodhaven." Nurse Higgins gave an endearing, gap-toothed smile that took years from her square features as she lifted Nora's head to allow her a few sips of cool water. "Looks like you're going to pull through."

"Thank you," she whispered.

"Nora?" The wall of sheets was batted aside as if they barred the gates to a keep. Mercy, of all people, charged in like a battering ram beribboned in sapphire silk.

"Nora, *thank God.*" She made her way to the bedside, clutching at the headboard and hovering as if she wanted to do something but couldn't figure out what. "Are you in very much pain? Do you require anything? Please don't fret. Pru and Morley will be here in..." She checked the silver watch she kept on a chain in the pocket of a velvet cobalt vest. "Four minutes ago." Her dark gold brows drew together. "Odd, it's not like them to be late."

As was often the case, Felicity followed in Mercy's wake, though she hung back, clutching a book to her chest as if it could shield her from conversations with people.

"Traffic on the bridge is insufferable this time of day," she managed helpfully before flushing scarlet when she noticed Mercy, Titus, Nora, and Nurse Higgins all turned to listen to what she'd said.

As Felicity held the sheet aside with one hand, Nora was able to see past her to what she noticed was only one rather large but ramshackle room. A waiting area consisted of six chairs in a circle, one of which was just vacated by a roughshod woman who was helping the man with his arm in a sling out the door.

The proximity to the windows told her she might occupy one of two or three beds in the entire place.

She blinked back to Titus, who lingered at the foot of her bed, having made room for her sisters to stand opposite Nurse Higgins.

It distressed Nora to find him in such a dilapidated clinic. With his brilliance, he could have secured a dignified position anywhere in the Empire. He'd such dreams when they were young, such ambitions. To alleviate suffering. To fight disease. To advance scientific medicine.

Well, they were neither of them young anymore.

She'd always hoped that life had been kinder to him, because of what she'd done.

And now, it seemed, even that hope was dashed.

Hot tears stung her eyes and, for the first time since

she'd awoken, she was glad he wouldn't look directly at her.

Apparently interpreting her expression incorrectly, Mercy repeated, "Are you in very much pain?" She looked imploringly up at Titus. "Should we give her something?"

Nora was in enormous pain, but it had less to do with her shoulder than the aching heart beneath it. "I-I'm all right, Mercy." She managed, with great effort, to lift her cheeks into the weak semblance of a smile. "I'd like to clear my head a little, I think."

"I agree that's best," Titus addressed Mercy rather than her, directly, as if her vivid sister could act as a conduit between them. "Though if the pain becomes untenable, I've found it can hinder healing."

"So, don't you suffer needlessly," Mercy ordered, stroking a lace glove over her hair.

Oh no. Her hair. Nora swallowed a pained groan. She couldn't bear to imagine what she looked like, and with her first love looming over her like some disheveled Adonis.

It shouldn't matter. But it did.

"Can you believe this is *the* Titus Conleith who used to work at Cresthaven?" Mercy presented him with the ease of someone who'd become well acquainted whilst she was asleep. "He saved your life not once but twice! Surely you remember, Nora? He and Felicity used to exchange books, and sometimes he'd carry our things out on picnics and shopping."

Nora's stomach turned abruptly sour at the words. Even as they'd carried on together, she'd treated him like the servant he was. He'd saddled her horses and carried her parcels, and she'd taken the assistance for granted.

"I remember everything," she whispered, hoping the hollow note in her voice didn't reveal her.

His expression never changed, though the hand that

had been resting on the iron footboard of her bed now tightened.

Felicity, dressed in a more subdued blue gown than her twin, adjusted her spectacles before reaching down to brush tentative fingers over Nora's hand. "Do you remember what happened before you were…injured?"

A dreadful gravity washed her in pinpricks of pain, starting at her scalp and trickling down her spine to land in her gut. "William…"

She couldn't force any more words around the growing lump of emotion in her throat.

If her father was the architect of her misery, then William was the engineer. For over a decade, he'd hurt, manipulated, and humiliated her. He had killed five men because Nora had allowed them to touch her.

Thank God he hadn't known about Titus. *Thank God. Thank God.*

"They cremated your late husband's remains," Felicity said gently, "and I took the liberty of having them interred at the family cemetery in Shropshire, without much ado."

Nora started, then winced as the slightest movement sent a burning sort of pain through her shoulder. "How long have I been here?"

"Four nights," Mercy answered.

"We've been taking turns watching over you so Dr. Conleith can see to his other patients, but he examines you every morning and is here every evening." Felicity dared a glance up at him before her gaze darted away. "And we all meet here for tea or supper, just as Dr. Conleith does his final rounds."

Nora did her best to blink away confusion. "We all?"

Mercy gestured expansively to the clinic at large. "Felicity, Prudence, and Morley, of course. Did you know he and Dr. Conleith fought in the war together?"

"Morley did most of the fighting," Titus said with a self-effacing grimace. "I was merely a medical officer."

He was never *merely* anything.

Nora had known he'd left Cambridge for a while before returning, but she hadn't discovered why until now.

Had war crafted the boy she'd loved into this man of brutal strength and sinew? Had it hardened his gentle eyes and deepened the brackets beside his mouth?

"I'm touched," Nora whispered. "That you were all here by my side, despite..." Despite the damage her husband had wrought on the entire family.

"Of course we were!" Mercy exclaimed. "Nora, had we known what William was like. What you had to endure—"

"Mercy." Felicity seized her twin's hand, looking as if she wanted to brain her sister with the tome she still held. "Let's not speak of that now, she's only just regained consciousness."

"Right." Chagrined, Mercy dropped her hands to her sides and clutched at her skirts as if she could contain herself that way.

"Mama and Papa send their...good wishes," Felicity said with an unconvincing smile. "They'll be ever so relieved to hear that you're out of the proverbial woods."

Would they be? Nora wasn't so certain. It might have been easier for them if she and William had *both* perished on the docks.

They could bury her shame forever.

Mention of the Baron and Baroness of Cresthaven seemed to galvanize Titus into action. He pulled a notebook from a pocket hanging at the foot of her bed. "The bullet created a small tear in your axillary vein, through which you lost a great deal of blood," he informed the notes as he flipped through them with industrious fervor. "That can be blamed for your lengthy lack of consciousness.

89

However, there have been no signs of further bleeding nor infection. I see no reason you cannot return to Cresthaven Place tomorrow to recover. I'll send notes and diagrams of my surgical repair for the attending doctor and—"

"Actually." Mercy held up a finger as if trying to get the attention of a teacher in class, though she looked nonplussed when it worked.

As if she didn't want to say what came next.

"Father mentioned… well, he thinks it's best you do not convalesce at Cresthaven Place. Not until William's crimes are all uncovered, and the extent of the scandal is known. There was no talking him out of it. You know how he is."

After so many years, her parents' lack of concern shouldn't hurt so much.

And yet…

Nora sighed. Perhaps she'd woken up too soon, after all. "It's all right. I would like to sleep in my own bed before I have to relinquish it to whomever will become the next Viscount Woodhaven."

"Do you know who that will be?" Mercy asked with an anxious wrinkle between her brows.

"I haven't the faintest idea. William had no siblings nor cousins, and was still convinced that I'd eventually give him an heir."

A soft clack rang in the silence that followed, sounding very much like teeth crashing together. Had that vein been so prominent in Titus's forehead before?

Mercy blew a ringlet away from her eye. "I hope he's not some strident old grump with a shrew for a wife. They can't take your rooms in town, can they? I mean, you're allowed a dowager stipend, are you not?"

Nurse Higgins adopted a rather protective posture over Nora, eliciting from her the most ridiculous urge to crawl into the matronly woman's lap and sleep for days.

"Now inn't the best time to be concerning her ladyship with such things, child," she gently reproached.

Sufficiently chastised, Mercy winced. "You're right, of course. Do forget all about it, Nora. I'm certain it'll work out."

Nora closed her eyes, wishing for all the world that Titus was not here to witness this. Did he know about William's crimes? About the wrongs she'd committed and the lovers she'd taken?

Likely.

She didn't care who the next Viscount Woodhaven was. She pitied him. All her husband had left him was a title tainted by scandal and weighted by untold debts.

"I—I should like to go home," she said, hating the plaintive wobble in her voice.

"That won't be possible, I'm afraid." A second masculine voice announced the arrival of Nora's recently acquired brother-in-law, Sir Carlton Morley.

He'd pulled the sheet behind Titus aside, and held it so his wife could duck around and rush to Nora before he reached out to greet Titus with a firm and familiar handshake.

Prudence, striking in a fitted day dress striped with gold and burgundy, took her place next to Nurse Higgins on Nora's uninjured side.

"There's so much to say," she whispered, kissing Nora's knuckles in a very uncommon display of affection for members of the Goode family.

Prudence had always been like that, however. Just a flower in need of rain, one who'd bloomed beneath her husband's protective, demonstrative care.

"Why can't Nora go home?" Mercy asked, cutting to the salient point as she was wont to do.

Though Titus stood a few inches taller than Morley, the Chief Inspector maintained the air of a man who commanded not only a room, but the largest and most organized police force in the civilized world. His midnight blue suit turned his glacial eyes an impossible, arresting color, and, unlike Titus, his cravat was perfect and not a single strand of fair hair would dare disobey.

The Chief Inspector was a famously contained man, but he'd demonstrated that his heart was true, and his love ran deep. He'd been prepared to die for Pru.

He'd killed for her without hesitation.

Nora wondered if he blamed her for her husband's actions. If he suspected her of involvements in William's crimes. As it was, his sharp, angular features were softened with concern as he delivered distasteful news with care. "We obtained a warrant to search your house for evidence of your husband's cohorts, and we found it ransacked."

A sudden dizziness had her tightening her grip on Prudence's hand. "Was anyone hurt?"

"No. Needless to say, your butler's resigned his position, as have your housekeeper and several other staff. It's not safe for you to return home, Lady Woodhaven."

A sudden headache stabbed Nora behind the eye, and her shoulder throbbed in earnest now, a burning pain adding to her discomfort.

But she'd been hurt plenty of times, and had to pretend that everything was fine.

She could do it now.

"What cause have you to worry that the burglars will return?" Nora asked.

He glanced at his wife, who threw warning daggers at him with her eyes.

"Tell me," Nora demanded. "I must know."

"There...was a note left by the invaders," Prudence conveyed with palpable reluctance. "One demanding the crate that William had apparently neglected to deliver to them. They threatened to take it out of his flesh, Nora.

Who is to say if they'll come for you now that he's..." She didn't say the word *dead*.

"Lady Woodhaven." Morley clutched the lapel of his coat, the only sign he had to fortify himself for the next question. "Do you know where your husband hid that money?"

"There's never *been* any money," Nora croaked, her anxiety dashing to the surface. "I'd taken to selling my jewels to pay the staff, and William squandered whatever salary he drew from the shipping company. He bragged that his newest venture was profitable, but I never saw the proof of it. I didn't believe him, all told."

She'd thought this was over. That she was finally free of him. How typical that even in death he could still threaten her safety and any chance at peace or happiness.

Morley's critical assessment was more invasive than any medical examination she'd endured, but she was too tired and soul-weary to be troubled by it. "You truly have no idea who would be after your husband?"

Nora searched the white sheet draped as a canopy above her bed for answers, noting some of the plaster from the ceiling had dislodged and peppered shadows on the fabric. No doubt, the reason the canopy was hung in the first place. "I knew he had a new venture, but he wanted to keep his whereabouts a mystery to me, and I didn't care to pry. I was stupid, I realize, but whatever took him away from the house...I encouraged it."

Her voice broke on the last word, not from tears but from fighting increasingly unrelenting pain. Her breath began to catch in spasms as a burning sensation ripped through her shoulder with gasp-inducing zings.

This was all too much.

"She's had quite enough," said Titus, accepting a cool cloth from Higgins and crowding her family away. Towering over her, he bent to wipe a sheen of sweat from her brow and upper lip.

93

When he brought his face close like this, she could see every striation of metallic beauty glimmering in his eyes. She could make out the variations of color in his shadow of a beard.

She could marvel at the feel of a gentle hand on her brow. How novel it was. How necessary.

"Morley, you can interrogate her some other time. She's in too much pain to be of use to you now," he ordered.

Nora gaped up at him. How did he know she was in pain? She'd been so careful not to let on.

Because he was a good doctor. Probably the best.

"She'll come home with us," Prudence declared. "If these cretins are after her, then she should be somewhere she's safe until Carlton has dealt with them."

Nora shook her head, her stomach curling in relief to see that Nurse Higgins had passed Titus a syringe filled with welcome oblivion. "Your house is the first place they'd look for me after Cresthaven, Pru. I won't put you and the Chief Inspector in danger."

At that, Morley let out an undignified snort. "I'm entirely capable of protecting those in my own home."

"But you cannot shirk your duties at Scotland Yard on my account," she argued. "You'll be away from home even more often if you're personally after the brigands my husband apparently stole from."

His expression was captured on the border between quizzical and offended. "I happen to know more than a few dangerous men who could keep you and my wife safe when I'm at the Yard."

She turned to the head of the Morley family. "Pru, you're with child. And until we know who my enemies are or how many—"

"She'll recover at my clinic in Knightsbridge," Titus announced before deftly sliding the needle into her arm and depressing the much-needed opiate into her vein.

Still, he refused to look her in the eye.

"You have a clinic in Knightsbridge?" Felicity asked from beside Nora, as agog as the rest of them.

Titus's chin dipped in a curt nod as Morley elucidated. "The good doctor is one of the most prolific and progressive surgeons in practice today. Hospitals and universities alike are clamoring for his expertise, but he's insisting on being a man of the people. You're lucky, Lady Woodhaven, that this new charitable venture of his was operational, or I don't know what we'd have done."

"How impressive, Dr. Conleith," Felicity marveled, staring up at him as if he'd hung the moon.

He took the needle from Nora's arm and replaced it with a cloth, holding pressure there for a moment as he crooked a lip in Felicity's direction. "I've told you to call me Titus, like in the old days."

Nora almost burst into tears at the way a touch of warmth laced his voice with velvet.

It would be what she deserved, to have to watch him fall in love with sweet, young, *darling* Felicity. They had so much in common. They were both so true of heart and she was... well she was many things now.

An invalid. An adulteress. The penniless widow of a murdering thief. Barren, ill-used, and contaminated by scandal. She'd been barely younger than Felicity was now when she'd loved Titus.

When he'd loved her, in return.

They spoke around her as the medication pulled her back down into the void, their voices urgent and quiet at the same time.

A hollow ache lodged within her that the medicine could never touch.

Why would he keep her under his roof when he could barely bring himself to look at her?

WARLORDS AND DRAGONS

W hat had he been thinking, insisting Nora stay beneath his roof when he could barely bring himself to look at her?

It was a question Titus asked himself every time he had to endure her presence on his examination table.

For twenty-three days, four hours and—he checked his watch—sixteen minutes, he had felt like some sort of mythic dragon with a captive maiden locked in his tower.

He didn't want to see her.

And yet, he'd become a hollow sort of fiend at the thought of never seeing her again.

Initially, he'd assumed that in the five-story Gregorian mansion he'd turned into a private surgery facility, Nora would be easy to both protect and avoid.

Stashed in his personal suite situated in the lush living quarters on the top floor, she'd have her every physical and medical need addressed by an army of staff, and she would only require his presence to see to her post-surgical care in decreasing increments until she was healed.

It was the least he could do, under the circumstances.

For his part, Titus's hours were so occupied, he barely had time to sleep, let alone think of her.

At least, that was the lie he told himself.

Using his current clinic to finance the start of five others dominated his every waking hour. He and Higgins visited at least one in each borough before the sun came up, and another at sunset, so they could spend the bulk of their time here at the Alcott Surgical Specialty Hospital.

He'd unfolded a cot in the corner of his first-floor office, and had defended the decision to Higgins's raised eyebrows thusly, "It's nearer the entrances in case of emergency, and deucedly convenient. I can't imagine why I haven't done so before."

She'd pursed her lips and rolled her eyes, wisely neglecting to mention his guest rooms upstairs.

He *didn't* have to remind her that to sleep in the same house as their guest would be scandalous and inappropriate.

To which she *didn't* reply that no one in the world knew the former Viscountess of Woodhaven was in residence, and that she couldn't possibly be the subject of more scandal than she currently was.

And he *didn't* tell her to mind her own bloody business.

Though he did employ orderlies and security on his staff, he still felt it necessary to keep an eye on things. If someone was coming for Nora, they'd have to get through him and a bevy of sharp implements first.

It was the dragon in him that made such foolhardy decisions. The same one that blazed with the instinct to wrap himself around her and breathe fire on whomever would put her in danger. He'd done so in many an exhaustion-induced dream.

But he woke to reality—and an aching back—each morning. And in said reality, he was no dragon.

And she was no maiden.

Which was why he never allowed himself to be alone with her. When Nora wandered down to the surgery as she did every evening, he made certain she was accompanied by one of her sisters, or Higgins. Titus would check her wound in this partitioned examination room, divulge the prognosis and progress, and then leave her to dress and be escorted discreetly back.

Because he couldn't trust himself to remember what sort of woman she truly was. A victim. A liar. A patient. A lover. A formative portion of his past he'd done his utmost to turn his back upon, lest he become lost to bitterness and regret.

Yes, to invite her here was to court trouble. Not only because she might be in danger, but because, despite everything, he'd come to live for these moments with her.

Moments when his fingertips found her flesh and the contact electrified him like nothing and no one else on this planet.

A doctor shouldn't feel like this, he reprimanded himself.

Shouldn't enjoy the silken strands of her hair as he pushed the midnight curls aside. Shouldn't thrill to the undoing of the intricate silk-covered buttons of her nightdress, if only to expose something as innocuous as her shoulder blade.

People were just parts. Just machines of intricate design, and he was like a machinist. A student of whatever chaotic engineer crafted such imperfect structures capable of miraculous feats of healing. He wondered sometimes that a supposedly benevolent being might build such an instable system that one tiny shift in the mechanisms and the entire thing turned on itself.

But Nora.

She'd always been something more. She wasn't simply an apparatus, she was a work of fucking art. In a world where nothing seemed to shock or thrill him, where he'd thought himself incapable of incredulity anymore. Just the sight of the improbable precision of her symmetry struck him with a sense of awe he hadn't known since he was a child discovering the newness of the entire world.

It affected him tonight just as utterly as it had done on the night he'd brought her here. Even though they'd both endured this odd routine for over three weeks, each time she appeared on his examination table elicited a strange sort of tremulous emotion. Something caught on the border of anticipation and antagonism.

Today, Mercy had kept Nora company, and was now holding a lively chat with Higgins as he examined Nora's shoulder from behind.

Titus enjoyed Mercy's company and appreciated her vivacity, especially now. She kept them from saying anything important to each other. Which was vital, because if he and Nora were alone, he might ask her why she seemed increasingly morose today.

And she might ask any one of the cryptic questions he'd seen lurking in the dark hollows of her eyes.

She might ask him what he thought of her, or how he felt. And he...hell, he couldn't answer that question in the mirror, let alone now. Furthermore, he wasn't about to unleash any sort of emotion on a woman who'd been through the trauma she had.

"Are you in pain?" he couldn't help but inquire.

"Very little," Nora replied, not even turning her head to address him.

"Is the mobility improving still?" He stabilized her shoulder with one hand, and lifted her elbow with the other, testing the movement. She winced a little, but not until they passed a threshold of motion greater than she had been previously capable.

"I see no sign of recurring inflammation and it seems the wound itself has achieved proliferation, at least superficially. I should think we could remove your stitches tomorrow."

"That is, indeed, a relief Dr. Conleith."

They were both so serene. So polite.

It was beginning to drive him mad.

"What is proliferation?" Mercy's inquisitive voice cut through the building tension as she leaned against the wall facing both him and Nora. She'd been tracing the cheek of an articulated skeleton he'd displayed in the corner, but dropped her hand and turned her full attention upon him.

"It's the stage of healing where new tissue forms along with vessels and sinew. It's too early for comprehensive proliferation, but we are well on our way. It will take the nerves the longest to heal, in my experience. But I'd say we are completely out of the woods."

Nora merely nodded her understanding.

"That's marvelous news," Mercy declared, adjusting her slim chocolate-colored vest and fluffing her cream lace cravat. She'd obviously spent a great deal of money to adopt the appearance of a student or an intellectual, including the adornment of wire-rimmed spectacles *sans* any lenses. A castoff of Felicity's, he'd wager. However, the garnets in the comb adorning her intricate coiffure, the matching ear bobs, and the sparkle of her watch undermined the effect. As did the fact that she was obviously educated more in the feminine arts than anything else.

She was a lovely girl if one was drawn to the wholesome vigor of youth, complete with wide oceanic eyes and gestures so animated as to be considered violent in some parts of the world.

"Felicity is pretending to take a nap as herself so she can accompany Mrs. Winterton on an errand as me, so I could come here alone," she announced, her wide mouth quirking with her specific sort of mischief.

"Why alone?" Nora asked her sister. "Mrs. Winterton is not so insufferable, as chaperones go, and seems to allow you both more freedoms than anyone they hired for Pru or me."

"Yes, well…" She darted an awkward glance to the far wall. "In light of recent events, Papa's rather put the lid on anything resembling freedom, I'm afraid. And today I'm intent upon attending a suffragist meeting."

At the mention of the scandal, Nora's bare shoulders visibly sagged, though her sister didn't seem to notice.

So that he didn't succumb to the temptation to comfort her, Titus said, "I don't know why you'd want to vote; politics is a terrible business."

Mercy's gasp conveyed a startling pitch for a surgery. "You don't *vote?*"

He shrugged. "You forget, I'm Irish and have no love for the government here. Besides, the parties are all corrupt and self-serving. In the end, they'll all send you to war to line their pockets. They'll all vote to occupy countries we have no cause to be in, whilst ignoring the immigrants and denizens of their own empire, who live in squalor and pain. Politics is a waste of my time, Miss Goode, when I have lives to save without much help from any politician."

At that, her lips twisted sardonically. "Well… if women voted, I'm certain there would be a great deal less war and a great deal more help for those in such need."

"Would that were true," he muttered. "But I don't see men allowing that to happen anytime in the near future."

Her eyes turned to chips of ice as she balled up her lace-gloved fist and punched her other palm. "Then we *make* it happen. We crush their opposition and bend their will until—"

"Careful. You're starting to sound like several warlords I know," he teased. "That's not very *merciful* of you."

Instead of taking offense, she threw her head back and laughed. "All of us are rather ironically named, it seems.

Prudence is often impulsive, Felicity is serious, I'm merciless and—" She stopped, gulping back the next words.

"And I am without honor," Nora finished without inflection.

"No!" Mercy knelt at her feet and snatched her hand. "No, no, no, that's not at all what I was—" Her features crumpled. "Oh, Nora, I *don't* think that about you. No one does."

Nora squeezed her sister's hand. "It's all right. Honor is…well it's difficult to define."

"At least none of us were named Chastity," Mercy grimaced.

Before Titus could consider her statement, Nurse Higgins charged into the examination room, saving anyone from having to reply. Her cap was uncharacteristically askew, and her cheeks as red as a ripe apple as she visibly seethed with wrath. "Mr. St. John is here again," she huffed. "He's demanding to see his wife. Has some papers she needs to sign, apparently, and when I told him she's not to be disturbed, he dispatched me to find my betters." She eyed him with mock disdain. "I suppose he means *you*."

Titus chuckled, used to the ribald banter he and Higgins enjoyed.

Elias St. John was a solicitor of no small means who'd often donated to the hospital. His wife was frequently ill and was often at the surgery being treated for a variety of ailments, from intestinal to nervous. One time, he had to operate a forearm snapped clean through.

A carriage accident, or so the police report stated.

"Inform him that Mrs. St. John is asleep. He can come back during visiting hours."

"He's threatening to take her home!" Higgins stomped her feet like a recalcitrant child.

"Impossible," he said, fighting to keep himself measured as he secured Nora's dressing. "The woman has an egregious head wound. She can barely stand without getting dizzy and falling over, nor can she feed herself through that broken jaw. I'm not releasing her until I'm certain she's out of the woods."

"If you send her back to that man, he'll kill her."

Titus's heart stopped and Mercy's eyes widened. "Nora? Did you just say…"

For the first time that evening, Nora craned her neck until her chin touched her shoulder, looking up at him with chilling certainty. "*He* did that to her."

Her words evoked that cold, bleak pain that lived alongside any other emotion regarding Nora. Twelve *years* of marriage to a man ultimately capable of attempting to take her life.

What else had she endured?

The question landed like a brick to the stomach every blasted day.

She rarely interacted with his patients, as they waited until visiting hours were over to attend her for the sake of discretion. So how could she know about Mrs. St. John's plight? Was this paranoia caused by a decade of mistreatment? Or…did she see something only a refugee of such a life could understand?

As a man who'd been to war, Titus knew that certain experiences could only be fathomed by those who'd shared them. Like Dorian Blackwell and those young lads who'd been locked in Newgate with him, or Morley and their blood-soaked battles together.

He finally looked her in the eyes, only to be unraveled by the beseeching look he found there.

"She won't survive the next time," she said with absolute conviction.

"I've thought it, meself," Higgins agreed. "There's something in that man's eyes makes me bones feel like they've been replaced by snakes."

As the surgeon, Titus rarely met his patients' families.

He'd simply performed Mrs. St. John's procedures and moved on to the next patient who needed him, letting his resident doctors and the head nurse deal with kin.

"Why did no one mention this sooner?" he demanded irritably.

"What would you have done?" Higgins eyed him as if his very gender made him dubious.

"I'd go to the police. Demand an investigation. It's been illegal to hurt your wife for a handful of years now, I think." How violence against a woman had ever been protected by law aggravated him in the extreme.

Higgins actually scoffed. "Men are never convicted without another male to bear witness. Women are rarely believed. They'd only send her home to him where he'd punish her for her trouble."

"We have to do something." Nora stood, suddenly animated, clutching the bodice of her nightshift to her bosoms with her one strong hand. "Mercy, aren't you and Felicity volunteers with the Duchess of Trenwyth's Ladies' Aid Society?"

"That's right!" Mercy snapped her fingers. "She oversees that sanctuary for women. I'm certain they'd help."

Titus nodded. "I know of the Duchess; she was once a nurse at St. Margaret's."

Nora turned to him, dark eyes wild. "Do you think Mrs. St. John could be moved without her husband's knowledge? She could hide, like me, until it's safe. She could divorce him."

Titus hesitated, quickly making some calculations. "If she'll agree to it, it could be done... gently. Though, I'll have to oversee it as I worry about transport with her head wound." He scrubbed a hand over his face, trying to wipe away fatigue. "Higgins, who can we spare to send to Trenwyth's to make arrangements?"

"I can go now!" Mercy's hand shot up like she was volunteering an answer in a classroom.

"What about your meeting?" he asked.

"Hang the meeting, this is more important. I'll go straight away and return with the news."

"Be careful," Nora admonished as she received a vehement kiss from Mercy, who turned to plant one ardently on Nurse Higgins's cheek on her dash out the door.

"Precocious child," Nurse Higgins chuckled, swatting at the air. "I'll go get rid of Mr. St. John, though I'd like to dump his arse in the alley with the rest of the rubbish."

"Like hell you will go out there." Titus dropped his arm like that of a bridge gate to block her. "If you consider him a dangerous or violent man, *I'll* get rid of him. You'll stay here where it's safe and see to Lady Woodhaven."

Higgins pushed against him, but he was planted to the ground, immovable as an old oak. "Don't be daft. He'd know something was amiss if the head surgeon came out to inform him of the visiting rules."

Nora's chest heaved with what he assumed was a multitude of emotion. "Men like him do not like to make a fuss in public. He'll be back tomorrow, trying a more manipulative tactic. He'll be as charming as you've ever seen," she predicted.

Higgins looked across at Nora, eyes soft in her uncompromising features. "You would know, child, as you had a bastard like that of your own to contend with."

Nora attempted a smile, as if she couldn't stand for her pain to be visible, but was unable to disguise it properly. "I'm two and thirty, hardly a child."

Higgins nodded, accepting that Nora didn't want her pity. "We'll save Mrs. St. John. Believe you me."

"Make certain you take that new orderly with you," Titus called.

"Very well," Higgins called back. "If only because you'll be an insufferable nag if I don't."

And then they were alone.

Titus looked around as if he might find someone to save him from her.

From himself.

All he found in the white examination room was an unhelpful skeleton…and the love of his life.

He raked a hand through his hair, scratching at his scalp. What…had just happened?

Nora began to struggle to pull her simple white nightgown up from the elbow of her injured arm with her other hand.

Galvanized, Titus went to help her, brushing her trembling hand aside so he could draw the sleeve over her shoulder in a way that didn't disturb it.

He stood behind her once again, sliding exactly one million silk buttons into place. All the while, he cursed every modiste and seamstress who decided anybody could sleep in such a silly contraption.

Silently, he lamented every slip of skin that disappeared.

"I would like to do something," she murmured.

His fingers stalled. "Anything in particular?"

She shifted with a restlessness he could sense growing in his own body. "I'm not used to being useless. I always have a charity for which to raise funds or some event to organize for…"

"For…" he prompted when she let the silence stretch for too long.

"For the Viscount," she mumbled before touching her chin to her shoulder to look back at him. "I've done nothing but read and visit with my sisters while I've been recovering, but I feel well enough to be up and about. Suppose I could sit with a few patients, or help some of the women through a hard row. I don't have anything in the way of medical training, but perhaps I could provide them comfort and understanding, like Mrs. St. John, for example."

How charming and lovely, that she desired to help. He understood her need to be useful, they were alike in that way. Compatible.

"I wouldn't be doing a very good job at keeping you safe and hidden if I paraded you around my surgery, now would I?" he asked, attempting to put her at ease without batting her idea out of the sky. "Your safety is paramount, but perhaps I can find you something to occupy your time so you don't go mad."

"You're kind." She turned to look straight ahead, and he wished he could read her expression. "Chief Inspector Morley will be here tomorrow. He sent a note saying he had news about my case…" She drifted off as he lifted her hair off of her neck and settled it down her back in a curtain of ebony silk. "Perhaps it's good news, and I'll no longer be your problem."

Was that what she was? A problem? A conundrum?

Something he had to figure out before he could sleep.

They stood like that for a moment, and Titus inhaled mightily, pulling the familiar scent into his lungs. She still used rose water, and smelled of a late-summer garden.

He became a hollow creature, only separated from the object of his yearning by the space of a breath.

And the chasm of a decade.

It was a heady torment. One he should want to be rid of.

And yet, the dragon within sought to roast Morley, as well, if he came to take her away.

He fought his curiosity as he secured her arm in the sling, enjoying the feel of her delicate limb as he arranged it against her chest before draping her cream dressing gown over her.

"Did Woodhaven…did he ever do something like that to you?" He shouldn't have asked that. He *couldn't* know the answer.

Because he couldn't kill the man twice.

INVISIBLE WOUNDS

itus had found no evidence of broken bones whilst treating Nora, and he'd looked for it. But there were other bruises, the ones in her expression.

"I don't want to speak of William," she said, pulling away.

Of course, she didn't want to discuss it, especially not with him. He should wish her good night, then. Should let her go.

"I'll see you back to your room." It was as if his mouth and brain were currently disconnected. They would be locked in the lift together. And then they'd come to his bedroom...

Christ, he'd never be able to spend another night there without thinking of her. No matter how often he washed the linens, he'd want to roll in them like a mad hound, searching for her scent.

He knew the impulse made him pathetic. He didn't bloody care.

Usually, he'd allow a lady to be first through a door, but he checked the deserted halls of his surgery before summoning her to follow him once he gleaned that the coast was clear.

They walked in silence down the hall, past the rows of

rooms wherein sleeping patients recovered from any myriad of operations from appendectomies to—God forbid—amputations.

Her slippers made no sound on the bare floors he'd ordered scrubbed twice daily. In the cream lace of her high-necked dressing gown, with her wealth of hair half unbound down her back, she resembled a ghost in the wan gaslight. A mere shade of who she'd once been.

She haunted his dreams often enough. His fantasies.

He doubted he'd be able to walk the halls of his own surgery without seeing the specter of her as she was just now. Pale and lovely. Sad yet serene.

She'd always moved with such innate grace, next to her he felt like a plodding draft horse. His heavy footsteps echoed along the empty hall as he took up entirely too much of it.

When they reached Mrs. St. John's room, she hesitated at the closed door. After looking in through the window upon the sleeping woman with naked anxiety, Nora turned to him, her expression troubled.

"Doctor Conleith..." she hesitated.

He should take back what he'd said before. Should insist she call him Titus. Everyone else in her family did.

But his name from her mouth... his breath became unsteady at the very thought.

It would be another thread of his own self-control, unraveled by her.

She shifted restlessly. "I feel compelled to thank you for—"

"You have," he interrupted brusquely. "Repeatedly."

"Not really," she contended, her gaze fixing on the bare forearms he'd crossed over his chest. "I know I've added my sentiments to my family's effusive gratitude. But in the weeks I've been here, I've not had the opportunity to express just how much I—"

"There's no need." For some reason, her gratitude rankled him. It was the last thing he wanted from her. They had any number of endless words to say to each other, and on the list he'd crafted in his mind, *thank you* didn't even make the first page. "Bullets are something of a specialty of mine, or *were*..." He drifted away, both verbally and physically as he turned toward the lift at the end of the hall.

He felt rather than heard her follow him. "You learned in Afghanistan?" she queried.

"I did."

"I always wondered why you went to war. I was told Dr. Alcott sponsored you to attend university."

It surprised him that she'd asked after him enough to have gleaned the information. The Goodes had not engaged Doctor Alcott for some time. "He did for a while, but he died of a sudden aneurysm. His family was not so keen on keeping up my education, and so I pledged my fledgling skills to Her Majesty's Army to further my experience in hopes of continuing my instruction."

"Did you suffer?" The whispered question was laced with such lamentable emotion, the fine hairs of his body vibrated with it.

"Everyone who goes to war suffers." Irked to find that the lift wasn't on the ground floor, he pulled the lever to call it down to them.

"Tell me?"

He looked at her askance. "Of my suffering?"

"If you wish. Just... tell me about you. About this." She gestured to the wide halls of his hospital. "About everything or anything."

Something hardened inside of him. Chafed and ached like an old scar in an approaching storm. "Why?"

"I've spent a decade wondering."

I've always been right here, he wanted to say. She could have found him any time.

He could only read her expression in silhouette; the

glow of the gaslights situated between each doorway illuminated a woman as resolute as she was curious.

She hadn't always been like that. And, it seemed, she'd the courage to fight battles of her own these days.

Don't make a fool of yourself by doing something so pathetic as begging, Titus. Her last words fell like shards of ice on the heart she'd begun to melt. *I can no longer stand the sight of you.*

"It was a short and savage war." His intonation had taken on some of that savagery, even as he endeavored to keep his register low for the sake of the patients. "There'd been a hailstorm of bullets on either side. The battles ground men into meat, and I spent my days like a butcher, white apron and all, covered in blood. I either dug bullets or shards of shrapnel from anywhere you can imagine, or hacked mangled limbs from screaming men."

"I can't imagine," she remarked, her brow pinched with what he dared interpret as regret. "I wonder that it didn't put you off of the entire business."

"On the contrary, I returned with a burning need to not only learn but improve our understanding of the surgical arts. I did whatever I had to, to make it through university, even going so far as to use my skills for rather nefarious people."

"The Black Heart of Ben More, I gather?"

His eyebrows lifted. "You know him?"

She lifted her good shoulder in a shrug. "Oddly enough, he's a former enemy of Morley's, and I take it that they're forming something of a friendship. It is no small wonder to Prudence. She speaks of it, often."

The lift arrived with a slight squeak. The intricate and decorative metal door folded in upon itself like an accordion as he pushed it aside for her.

Nora stepped past him, the scent of roses and warm female flesh beckoning him to follow.

He kept talking, doing his utmost to avoid any

fraught silences between them. "The army didn't pay enough for me to finish Cambridge, but Dorian Blackwell did. He needed a doctor in his debt to attend to his men without asking questions. I saved his eye back in the day…as well as I could. Now that he's gone mostly legitimate, I'm inclined to prevail upon his newfound generosity."

"Oh?" The question seemed to escape on a tremulous breath as he reached past her to depress the lever that would propel the lift up to the fifth floor.

As the blasted thing lurched to a start, she stumbled into him.

Reflexively, his arm went around her, pulling her to his side so she might use his sturdy form as a bulwark.

It had been a mistake, to press her soft curves against his hard angles. To fill his hands with her in the shadows.

If she wasn't a wounded woman, he might have taken the upturn of her face, the parting of her lips, as an invitation.

"I'm sorry. I'm not used to these contraptions. I'm rather uneasy to not find my feet on solid ground." She put her hand against his chest as if to push away, but it stayed there.

Right over his heart.

Could she feel it leaping behind the cage of his ribs? Hurling itself against her palm.

As if she hadn't held it since he was a lad of ten.

As if it couldn't wait to be broken again.

He released her instantly. What had they been talking about? Oh yes…

Money.

"I've sunk a fortune into this place because I couldn't stand to practice surgery in the hellholes they call hospitals here. I wanted a situation that was not only specialized, but clean, where patients had a greater chance of recovery, and it's succeeded. The infection rate is down, and the survival rate is so much higher than I even projected."

He watched the floors fall away with a glowing sort of pride in each one. "In my exuberance, I have endeavored to open many more like this. The surgery in Southwark, for example, where so many industrial accidents need seeing to. But I've overstretched, it seems. I'm often too busy performing actual procedures to raise funds. I've financed what I can… but it's rather taken on a life of its own. And there is always more need than there are those trained to fill it. I'd like to sponsor the education of young talent…"

The lift halted at the top floor, so he opened the cage and swept his hand for her to lead the way.

She didn't move. Merely looked at him with dark eyes shining in the lone dim lantern of the lift. "I'd give you my entire fortune if I had one," she said with a youthful earnestness that conjured that lively girl he'd once known.

He had to clear his throat before replying. "You are kind."

She shuffled past him, murmuring something that sounded like, "We both know I am not."

The corridors of his private residence were unnervingly silent. Not just because the plush carpeting muffled their footsteps, and velvety arabesque wallpaper dampened their acoustics. A strange expectancy emanated from the shadows in between the delicate gold sconces aligning the walls.

Their glow was dimmer than usual, gilding the atmosphere with more shadows than illuminations. Next to him, Nora was like a beacon, her gown a shock of light in the dark opulence, her hair an inky sheen around features that were the perfect paradox of soft and sharp.

Titus's heart gave an extra thump as his body responded to the proximity to her and to his bed.

Nothing could happen between them.

"Do you still like to ride?" she queried.

"Hmmm?" He wasn't certain he'd heard her correctly. Also, the word "ride" from her mouth instinctively tightened his cock against the placket of his trousers.

It had become a meaningful word to them in their youth. One with more salacious connotations, as they often used the excuse of riding to spend amorous time together.

"Do you remember how we used to fly along Rotten Row? I miss that. If I could have anything back, it would be the horses and...those afternoons."

"I hardly have the time for such things," he answered in a tone flat enough to draw her curious attention.

"It seems we should both relearn how to enjoy ourselves."

"I enjoy what I do."

"I can tell," she said, reaching out to run her finger along a small display table as they passed it. "But I imagine you should find some recreation, just as I should find something to give my life purpose."

You could work here with me. The words leapt to his lips and he swallowed them immediately. Too much. Too soon.

Or was it too little, too late?

"Where do you think you'll go after this is over?" he asked.

She lifted her hand and caught at a strand of her hair, worrying it with deft fingers. "Well, I'm too notorious to stay in London, I think. The papers have spilled every sensational detail of my life, along with my husband's innumerable crimes. There is a dowager cottage in the country that I might prevail upon, but...I recently spent some time in Italy and grew fond of it. I think of returning often. I like the sunshine there."

"Italy?" The very word offended him. "What the devil would you do in Italy?"

Approaching the door of his chamber, she stepped aside so he could rest his hand on the latch. "Men mistreat their wives everywhere. Perhaps I can be useful in that way. It could be a way for me to make reparations for whatever damage I've done."

What would be worse? To know she lived close? Or across a continent?

He reached out and covered the hand working tangles into her hair with his own, wanting to soothe whatever anxiety caused her to fidget.

"*I* never would have hurt you, Nora." It needed to be said. He couldn't fathom the reason, but there it was.

She faced him, the lamps glimmering off a sheen of moisture in her eyes as her hand stilled beneath his. "I've never feared you for a moment."

No creature should be so soft. So inviting.

The air thickened between them and Titus didn't know how they'd come to be closer to one another. Couldn't say which one of them had stepped forward to close the gap.

"Nora?"

Her tongue darted out, glossing her lips. "Yes?"

"If you knew what I'd become? If you'd seen this place and realized what I could have eventually offered you... would you still have thrown me out that night?"

He watched her features crumple and immediately regretted the question. Even though she'd been cruel in their past. Even though she'd been so contaminated by disgrace in the eyes of society for all her supposed misdeeds.

Even though he'd never truly forgiven her...

It seemed he'd still rather tear at his own skin than cause her pain.

To his surprise, her fingers laced with his and she

pressed lips as plush and smooth as petals to knuckles still rough from a youth spent in toil.

"Titus..." She swallowed twice before gathering herself to continue. "You were the brightest, best, most brilliant person I'd ever known. That I'd ever even heard of. I *always* understood you were capable of this and more. I never for a moment questioned that, unless you had the chance taken from you, you would perform miracles. You were born to astonish the world."

Pleasure shimmered through him at her words, followed by a dart of ire. "Then...why—"

"Titus?"

At the sound of his name, so familiar on another woman's lips, he dropped Nora's hand just in time for the bedroom door to open.

Revealing Mrs. Annabelle Rhodes.

Tossing her abundant copper curls, Annabelle pressed a hand to the deep cleft of her cleavage in a gesture meant to be both enticing and astonished. "It's been a *month* of Wednesdays since you've taken me up on my...invitations."

"Annabelle," he growled.

She drew her generous bottom lip between her teeth, her green eyes already hungrily devouring him. "Since you claimed to be too busy to leave your lair, I decided to join you in it. To steal whatever moments you can spare. I've been famished for—"

"Annabelle," he forced her name through his teeth. "I did not give you a key so you could—"

As she advanced out the door, she finally noticed he wasn't alone. Her eyes narrowed as she drew her gaze up and down Nora's dressing gown.

"Titus...who *is* this?"

"I'm no one, I assure you," Nora said from beside him, turning the arm in the sling to the light. "Merely a patient."

"A patient, you say?" Annabelle planted her fists on her buxom hips. "Then what are you doing in the doorway to his bedroom this time of the evening?"

Titus opened his mouth to put Annabelle in her place, but Nora stepped in front of him. "I'm Nora," she introduced herself in an endlessly pleasant voice. So cultured. So practiced. So false. "Dr. Conleith is an old friend of the family. I've been prevailing upon his hospitality whilst visiting London, but I'll be leaving in the morning when my family arrives to collect me."

Would she?

Annabelle's features positively melted with delight, and then sobered when she realized that it was her in the scandalous position. "Oh. Well... I'm also a patient, or rather, my husband was. He died. Not for any lack of expertise on the part of—"

"I understand," Nora said, rather kindly, he thought, under the circumstances. "I'll bid you both goodnight."

"But..." Titus made to take her elbow, but she backed out of his reach. She'd been sleeping in his chamber, the door of which was filled by his current mistress.

"Until tomorrow." She smiled pleasantly and curtsied with enough grace to please the Queen, before she turned away.

But not before Titus spied the falter in her smile. The crack in her façade.

Then, with her back as straight as any royal, she glided down the corridor and disappeared into the guest room furthest away from his chamber. Shut the door.

And locked it.

WILD BEASTS AND SAVAGES

*H*ad they? Or hadn't they?

The question burned a hole into Nora's brain through the entirety of the night. Slowly. Torturously. Like the dedicated beam of sunlight a cruel child would direct through a magnifying glass at an insect.

Nora did her level best to concentrate on the conversation with Chief Inspector Morley. She knew it was important, that it had to do with her immediate future.

But how could she focus on anything else without knowing if Titus had been inside his mistress last night?

The woman hadn't stayed over—thanks be to God—but neither had she promptly taken her leave. She'd remained shut in Titus's chambers for exactly forty and seven minutes.

Long enough for a frenzied tryst, though Nora heard no evidence of pleasure.

Thank heavens for small mercies; that might have done what the bullet had failed to and finished her off entirely.

Titus had not come to her after Annabelle left, and she hadn't truly expected him to. She had no claim upon his time, let alone his heart.

Or his body.

His lovely, long-limbed, exquisitely sculpted body.

But a kiss had haunted the space between them before they'd been interrupted. Or had she conjured that through wishful thinking?

Nora *hadn't* imagined the rather unmistakable outline of his aroused sex pressing against the fitted fabric of his trousers. His physique had been as taut and strong as she remembered, and responded to the feel of her just as it once did.

With hard male need.

And his dratted mistress had been served up to him on a buxom platter, all pouty lips and giant bosoms, *apparently* famished for him.

For his cock. That was what she'd been about to say...

Had he given it to her?

"Lady Woodhaven?"

Nora blinked against the late-morning light streaming in through the parlor window, somehow blindingly bright even though the sky was a dull silver-grey. She realized she squeezed the handle of her porcelain teacup hard enough to shatter it, and set it back on the delicate saucer.

"Forgive me, Chief Inspector, I haven't been sleeping. Could you repeat the question?"

Morley cleared his throat and divested himself of his coat. Draping it across the back of the gold damask chaise, he tugged at the thighs of his trousers to perch on the edge.

He assessed her from beneath brows only slightly darker blond than the hair he kept ruthlessly short and elegant, no doubt in a ploy to soften the brutal angles of his features. If there were a more perfect man for Prudence, she'd dare the devil to find him. He was all hard jaw and starched collars, where her sister was flowing ribbons and soft smiles.

She hoped he made Pru happy. He certainly seemed to.

"I asked if *the Fauves* means anything to you." He kept his question measured, but she had the impression he evaluated every single aspect of her reaction.

She searched her memory. "A French word, isn't it? Meaning beast? Wild beast?"

"What about Raphael Sauvageau?"

She shook her head. "Was William working for him?"

"My investigation has borne out that his is the fist tightening around the black market these days. And, for a while, his men were watching your house, and mine." His expression flattened to patently grim. "It seems you were wise to go into hiding as, the deeper I dig into this brigand's machinations, the more concerned I become. His gang of degenerates call themselves the Fauves."

"Have you connected him to my—to William somehow?" She'd stopped thinking of him as her husband ages ago.

Morley rubbed at his brow as if erasing a headache. "Several nights ago I—apprehended one of his men and gleaned that cocaine is the least of Sauvageau's concerns. As he told it, a shipment of unminted gold from America went missing while in your husband's possession. Sauvageau is lying in wait, it seems, certain that much gold can't stay hidden for long. To spend it, someone must smelt it. And if it were in your possession and you sold it...your influx of fortune would become readily apparent. I imagine that's why he's watching you."

"Well I'm in no danger of a fortune, apparent or otherwise." Nora put her tea and saucer back on the tray table at her elbow, and then smoothed the skirt of her cotton frock over her knees with a wry sound. "Do you remember at the docks, before I was..." She cleared her throat. "William was frantic over a missing crate. He was going to take Prudence and me somewhere downriver."

Morley shifted with consternation, turning to look out the window toward the district over which Harrods gleamed above London's wealthy merchant class. "I'd give my eyeteeth to know where the crate is now," he muttered as if to himself. He glanced back at her, his glacial eyes softening for a moment. "We haven't spoken of that day. You must have complicated—even hostile—feelings about what happened. About me."

"Why would I, Chief Inspector?"

He blinked thrice before answering. "I killed your husband. In front of you."

Nora shut her eyes.

Not because she harbored any unpleasant feelings... but because she didn't. Morley had done what she'd fantasized about more than once. What she'd never had the courage to do.

He'd saved Prudence, and for that she'd always consider him a hero.

He apparently mistook her silence for grief. "In my experience, women often still love the husbands who hurt them. Even after they've done their worst. There's no shame in that. I don't blame you if—"

"I never loved William," she said vehemently. "*Ever*. And I will be forever grateful to you for saving my sister's life. My husband was a monster and, apparently, a killer. When I think of all he did because of me..." Emotion choked the air from her throat and tightened her muscles in such a way that set her shoulder to aching. "I only wish I'd had the courage to put an end to him sooner."

"You'd have been hanged for murder."

"Better my life than those of the innocent men he killed."

He leaned forward as if he meant to offer comfort, and then thought better of it when he caught the look of caution in her eyes.

"What he did to your...lovers, was no fault of yours."

His eyes shifted away. "Tell me to mind my own business, but were you emotionally involved with any of them? Do you have...someone to turn to with your grief? I've always found Dr. Conleith to be a keen and considerate confidant—"

"Titus is the last man I'd discuss such matters with." Nora stood, pacing away from him toward the window, if only to retreat from her guilt.

"They were all kind men, even George, the philandering rake. Hadn't a mean bone in his body. But I...was with him because I knew I would never feel attachment to a man like him. Likewise, my time with the Stags of St. James was nothing more than selfish pleasure. A diversion I paid for so I wouldn't have the complication of emotion. None of them meant more to me than what we did in the darkness. Perhaps that makes me a monster, as well."

She looked at her reflection in the window, a translucent overlay against the skyline, and didn't recognize herself in it. "I mourn them. They were vital men who once *lived*, and because of my actions, they no longer do."

Morley approached her carefully, standing at her shoulder to survey the city he was sworn to protect. "As much as I'm glad I put William in the ground, I perversely understand the primitive need to kill a man for touching the woman you love. Only... most of us don't follow through on the instinct."

That he admitted his jealous nature made her smile for Pru's sake.

"But what I can't fathom," he continued, "is how you can love someone and wound them on purpose."

Titus's young face flashed before her mind's eye, his anguished expression at her long-ago cruelty wounding her a thousandfold.

"William only knew how to hurt what he loved," she said. "He didn't beat me, per se. Not with fists and rage and the hatred that I see some men unleash upon their wives. His love was obsessive. Cruel. It was as if he wanted to punish me for not loving him back."

For loving another, she didn't say.

Suddenly the tableau of the city melted away, and the years she'd spent with a madman played like a stereograph against the grey sky. "He toyed with me endlessly. Isolated me from having friends. Made me pay for every moment I didn't spend with him, even when I took a day out with my family. He would profess his effusive love for me, threatening to kill himself if I couldn't summon warmth for him. And then, when I tried, he would see through my pantomime of affection and would tell me how easy it would be to hurt me while I slept. Would explain in graphic detail what ways he fantasized about torturing me. Terror was his weapon of choice. There were weeks I didn't sleep for fear of what he'd do, certain that this was the moment he'd finally lose what was left of his mind."

"It is unfathomable that there is no legal recourse for such behavior." Morley's voice was a tangle of frustration, the heat of his breath lightly fogging the window in front of him. "I don't wish to prod at bruises, but William mentioned that he hurt you...physically. Was that a lie?"

Nora shifted with distress, but for some reason she wanted to say it. To tell someone what the last decade had been like without worrying about their resulting emotions. Morley was a perfect recipient of such information. He wasn't a squeamish man. He dealt with the worst humanity had to offer on a daily basis. And he'd secret shadows in his eyes that had been put there by someone volatile. Though it was difficult to imagine what could strike fear into a dominant, confident man like him, she knew he understood her sense of helplessness.

"William used to tell me he would someday disfigure me, but he never so much as slapped my face. He would throw things. Break things. He tripped me a few times, once halfway down the stairs. He'd push me into the sharp side of a table or a doorframe. It was all so childish, so retributive." She swallowed a familiar rise of revulsion. "Sometimes, he would hurt me at night...when we were together. If only to elicit a response from me, he'd say. It was the guilt he felt later that disgusted me the most. The weeping. The begging of my forgiveness."

"Christ," Morley hissed, his fists tightening at his sides. "It's no wonder to me, that you sought comfort in the arms of other men."

"Comfort was always elusive," she sighed. "But sometimes I found escape."

Her surprise at his easy acceptance of her scandalous behavior caused her to study him more closely. "How very progressive of you, Chief Inspector, to be so compassionate, even when my shame is another mark on your own wife's reputation. All of England knows I paid the Stags of St. James for pleasure. Even though innumerable men openly keep mistresses and courtesans at their disposal or wile their nights away in brothels, it seems a woman's desire is not to be tolerated."

He let out a rather undignified snort, a ribbon of color peeking above his collar and crawling toward his cheeks. "I'm hardly one to throw stones, my lady, glass houses and all that. Surely you know how Prudence and I met."

As if summoned by her name on his lips, Prudence threw the parlor door wide and swept in like an errant ray of sunshine in her buttercup yellow gown. "Look who I found lurking outside of the door," she said airily, leading an obviously reluctant Titus into the room by his elbow. "He said your stitches come out today, isn't that marvelous?"

"I was waiting for your conversation with Morley to finish," he muttered.

It only took one look into his blazing eyes to know that he'd overheard *everything*.

"I wish I had more to report," Morley lamented. "Raphael Sauvageau is in the wind as far as we know, but I have my best men on it."

"I have it on good authority that even the Knight of Shadows is searching for him," Prudence said with a conspiratorial gesture.

Morley sent his wife a quelling look. "We have no reason to believe that you're in immediate danger, as you are not spending a gangster's gold. However, it wouldn't be a terrible idea to remain here for the foreseeable future, if we might prevail upon the good doctor's generosity for a few days more." He turned to Titus with a familiar smile, one that stalled when he glimpsed his high color, tense jaw, and the dangerous gleam in his eye. "Unless…"

"Consider my generosity extended," Titus clipped, setting his medical bag on a decorative table with more force than was necessary.

Morley glanced back and forth between them for a moment, his shrewd gaze narrowing with suspicion and no little amount of concern. "Are you quite certain that—?"

"She stays." The way Titus stated the directive stirred something low in Nora's belly. He was a man of unfailing consistency, but something masculine and fierce shimmered in the air around him, even as he stood unnaturally still and contained.

For the first time she could remember, he seemed unpredictable.

It occurred to Nora to be afraid, but the fear never rose within her.

Not of him. Never of him.

Prudence went to her husband and took the arm he offered. "Best we take our leave, darling, so Nora can prepare to have her wound seen to." She bustled Morley toward the door, but not before arching a meaningful brow at Nora that said she would be asking questions about Doctor Titus Conleith at the first available moment.

"Yes, well, I'll be in touch." Morley slapped Titus's shoulder on the way out, but he didn't seem to notice.

He just stared at her without blinking, looking for all the world like a man who'd been punched out of the blue, and was shaking off the astonishment before winding up to throw his own fist.

"Do you need assistance with your buttons?" he queried through clenched teeth.

Her knees quivered, but not for the reason one might have assumed. "No. I can manage."

Nora turned away from him, back toward the window, and lifted her fingers to the buttons of her bodice. Even though she still wore her sling most of the day, he'd encouraged her to use her arm to strengthen it, including getting dressed in the morning. She'd abandoned the sling for tea with Morley, and still felt fairly well off without it.

She'd only sent for dresses that buttoned up the front and—since she'd thought it unfair to ask a lady's maid to hide away with her—generally prevailed upon one of her sisters to arrange her hair in a loose braid down her back.

As she gingerly shucked the bodice down her shoulders, she felt more exposed in her chemise and loose, low-slung corset than she had certain times when she'd been nude.

It might have been the way Titus's gaze snagged the edge of her corset, where it barely came high enough to cover her nipple. He immediately looked away, his gaze affixing to some distant point behind her as a vein appeared on his forehead.

"You'll excuse me for not attending to this earlier. I was escorting Mrs. St. John to Lady Trenwyth's." He made a terse gesture for her to sit on the chaise before him, which she did. "Higgins is still there getting her settled," he offered by way of explanation as he rummaged in his bag for a minuscule yet wickedly sharp pair of scissors.

He pulled the table in front of her forward and perched on the edge. Their knees had to mingle in between each other's in order for him to get close enough to reach her stitches.

She tried not to notice the outline of his thighs against the fabric of his trousers.

Despite his apparent ire and sharp, jerky motions, he was infinitely gentle and precise as he snipped through the stitches on her shoulder and plucked them out with clever metal tweezers.

He'd brought the scent of the city indoors with him, soot and the hint of crisp air as summer gave way to autumn. The aromas underscored other fragrances she was beginning to associate with him. Something sharp and clean, like stringent soap softened by the camphor-like essence of his aftershave.

He was fastidious with his hygiene, his teeth clean and cared for, his thick hair tamed by pomade, at least in the mornings. By this time in the afternoon, that wicked forelock, the color of burnt caramel, escaped to brush his eye, making him appear even younger than his thirty years.

Her fingers itched to smooth it out of his warm whiskey eyes. To trace the topography of his stern features with a cartographer's fervor. To rediscover terrain she'd mapped just over a decade ago. Not just with her fingers, but with her lips, as well.

She wondered if he tasted like he used to.

Her mouth watered so violently her cheeks stung with it.

"Thank you for seeing to Mrs. St. John with such

alacrity." She lowered her chin, tilting her head as if she might catch his gaze.

It remained firmly upon her shoulder as he worked.

"It is my responsibility to look after my patient's well-being. Your gratitude isn't necessary." He discarded the last of her stitches onto a tray and stood, stepping around to stand at her back, where he expertly went to work on the exit wound.

A rebellious ire welled within her breast, overflowing until she thought she might choke on it.

What had he to be so annoyed about? He'd the perfect chance to be rid of her, and he'd insisted she stay. She'd not embarrassed him in front of his paramour, which had been utterly well done of her, considering that she'd been tempted to scratch the woman's eyes out. So, what had ignited his remarkably long fuse?

With each stitch he pulled free, that much more of her self-containment was likewise undone, until, when he set his instruments down on the tray with a clatter, she could contain herself no longer. "I'm enjoying your hostility today. It's quite naked."

His exhale contained the long-suffering of every man who'd ever been trapped alone in a room with a confounding woman. "I'm not hostile. I'm aghast. For the past decade, I'd accepted that I'd been thrown over so you could be the woman you were portrayed as in the society papers. The ideal aristocrat. The *ton's* true beauty. Woodhaven was your cousin of some distance. Did you not realize what kind of man you were marrying? Did you understand what being a Viscountess would cost you?"

For reasons inexplicable, his questions enraged her.

"I didn't marry William to be a Viscountess. I married him because—" She couldn't say it. Even when they were angry with each other, she couldn't lay the blame at his feet. Because it didn't belong there. Not really.

She'd made the choice, even though she'd done it to

save him from her father. She burned to tell him that. But what good would that cruelty do now?

"I married William because he was chosen for me. And we got on nominally well at first. He didn't show me his true self until a year had passed, and by then it was too late. He was a small, bitter man. And so, yes, I resigned myself to my fate as his wife. I endured his tortures and his spite. I advanced his position in society as hostess. I covered up his indiscretions—"

"Not without committing indiscretions of your own," he muttered.

Antagonism drove her to her feet, and she whirled to face him. "How *dare* you condemn me for that. You haven't exactly been a monk, or have you already forgotten your time alone with the shapely widow, Mrs. Annabelle Rhodes, just last night?"

His frown deepened to a scowl, but he remained silent as he gathered the paper he'd placed her stitches on and folded it, presumably for the rubbish bin.

Her eyes narrowed. "I've known a few hypocrites in my day, but I'd never imagined you were one of them."

He dropped the paper on the tray, shadows gathering on his features like ominous storm clouds. "I didn't touch Annabelle last night. I ended it with her."

Nora expelled a breath she hadn't realized she'd been holding since meeting the woman. But the information, welcome as it was, didn't douse her ire. "Well, I haven't touched a man for ages, and yet you're still obviously upset."

"Not about—that isn't what I—" He broke off with a growl, wrapping his instruments in cloth and tossing them back in his bag. "I don't condemn you for having... needs. But the Stags of St. James, Nora? You would pay *prostitutes*?" He squared his shoulders to her, his chest heaving as his volume increased. "For Christ's sake, you carried on an affair with the man who would become your sister's fiancé—"

"Only because they looked like you!"

He froze.

She clapped her hand over her mouth. But it was too late.

The truth had already escaped.

"What...are you saying?" His broad shoulders were bunched, straining against his shirtsleeves, his skin white over clenched knuckles. He was assembled like a sleek and predatory cat, his muscles gathered as if he might lunge.

Or flee.

Nora's own breath sawed in and out of her as if she'd run a league, but now that it had been said, the rest of it tumbled out of her like an avalanche of truth. "They were all tall, strong, and brutally handsome, with umber hair and...coarse hands. That's what I looked for when I selected a lover. Square, capable hands like yours, rough from working. It didn't matter what color his eyes were because I would... turn out the lights. Would make them be silent. Like we were the night we were together."

"Nora." Her name escaped him like a warning. Or a plea. His expression caught somewhere in between torment and relief. He shook his head, slowly, but she didn't know what he meant by it.

And she couldn't seem to stop herself now.

"You said *nothing* that night," she marveled, much as she'd done so many times in the years since when she'd taken the memory of their first time together to cherish. "You asked no permissions and you offered no effusions. You just knew what I wanted, and you gave it to me. We just...*existed*. And it was perfect. So, every man I paid, any lover I took, any time I found completion beneath someone's body, I—" She broke away, her jaw working to the side as she grappled with emotion too powerful to suppress any longer.

"It was all a parody. A shadow of what we'd done. Of what I wanted—yearned for—every night of my life, thereafter. I took others to my bed to erase the memory of what my husband did to me, but in my mind. In my heart. I never made love to anyone but you." She ventured forward, reaching out for him. Feeling bare and raw and exceedingly vulnerable.

"Don't." He held up a hand, effectively freezing her in place with her arm still outstretched. Her silent plea for comfort unheeded. "Don't you *fucking* dare," he seethed, pinning her with an accusatory glare before storming past her toward the window. "Don't take my anger from me, Nora; it's all that's kept me sane. The only thing that stopped me from blasting down the door at Cresthaven, throwing you over my shoulder, and abducting you to some place they never would have found us."

If only he would have. If only...

She turned to find his back to her, so broad and straight, the striations of his muscles visible even against the silk of his vest. But it was his reflection in the window that arrested her gaze. The agony in his eyes that broke her heart.

"God, all I can think about is the hell of your wedding night. I've never been so bloody drunk. I couldn't endure the fact that you belonged to another man, that someone *else* was inside of you."

"It was no picnic for me, either, if that helps ease your mind."

"Of course, it bloody doesn't!" he exploded, slamming his palm on a table beside him before whirling back to her. "And yet you *chose* him, Nora. After I gave you pleasure. I worshiped every inch of you until you were begging for me. I loved you, goddammit. You *know* I did. And

131

you *chose* that...that..." He couldn't seem to land on a word foul enough to encompass her late husband.

And she couldn't blame him.

"You can't know for sure that you loved me," she whispered.

He pinned her with a glare that would have made the devil himself cower. "How could you dare doubt it?"

She shook her head, aching for him, but also realizing something for the first time. "I do not doubt that your feelings were pure. But like everyone else, you loved a construct. An image of perfection manufactured by your own desires and my fabricated behaviors. You loved your idea of who I was. Because you didn't know me, Titus. No one ever has."

He crossed his arms over his chest. "Who are you then, Nora?"

At that, she stalled. "I—I..." She could not give him a complete answer, because she didn't know it herself.

Who am I? Shouldn't someone know that by two and thirty? When everything was stripped away. The title and the artifice. The scandal and the secrets.

What was left?

"You think I didn't see through you, even then?" he challenged, visibly struggling to regain his composure. "That I didn't know exactly who and what you were. You were never faultless, but Christ, to me you were perfect. I loved you *for* your flaws, not because I was blind to them. And I never would have punished you for being who you are." He stared at the puckered skin where the bullet had pierced her, and it throbbed in response to the pain underscoring the fury she read in his expression.

"Everything he did to you. Every way he made you suffer. Holy God, Nora." He laced his fingers in his hair and pulled as if he could tear a thought out of his mind. "I would have...I would have *killed* him for you, you know that? The moment he touched you, at the first cruel word.

If you would have come to me, I would have broken every oath I'd taken to do no harm, and I would have butchered the man."

He shook his head, his gaze a well of fathomless misery. "Can you imagine how it feels to know the privilege of spilling his blood went to Morley when I would have *bathed* in it, Nora? I would have smeared it on my skin like some primitive, clannish ancestor, and torn at his beating heart with my teeth—"

"No." She rushed forward, pressing her fingertips to his mouth, hot tears streaming from her eyes. "No, that isn't you. That isn't who you are."

He caught her wrist but didn't move it or toss it away. Instead he turned his cheek into her palm, the stubble of his jaw abrading her with vibrations she felt all the way up her arm. "It seems neither of us knows the other. Not anymore. But I know my mind, Nora. I always have done. I know what I am. I know what I want. And all I've *ever* wanted, was you." His eyes hardened in tandem with his voice. "And *you*..." He released her hand, visibly locking down, pulling up the ramparts and closing the gate.

"No," she cried, panicked. She wanted this. This honesty. His pain. She wanted him to lash her for what she'd done to him. If ever there was a punishment she deserved, this was it. "What? *What?* Tell me what I've done."

"You fucked them!" he roared. "You fucked *them* when I was here all along. I was *here*, Nora... I was right. Fucking. Here!"

He seized upon a crystal paperweight and wound his arm to smash it against the wall.

But he didn't.

He locked his long, talented fingers around it as if he could crush the crystal, filtering a snarl through a tight throat. After a few heaving breaths, he placed it back where it belonged.

Safe. Unbroken.

Just like she'd predicted he would. Because he was wrong about one thing.

Nora knew him.

He didn't break things or people, he repaired them. He always had. He didn't act without consideration. Even when every primitive instinct that made him so completely male, howled at him to rend and destroy.

He was better than that.

Better than any man she'd ever known.

Most certainly better than her.

"I had hoped you'd moved on," she confessed woodenly. "I didn't come to find you because I'd anticipated that you'd found a way to be happy. How could you not when you're so easy to adore? I could not add interrupting that happiness to my list of many sins. I couldn't do that to whomever loved you, any more than I could watch you love someone else. Or see the babies you might have put inside of her—"

He seized her then, tenderly, passionately, his hands bracketing her face, cradling it as if it were a precious, breakable thing, even as he delivered crushing blows with his words. "There's no one. There has never *been* anyone else. I always realized it made me pathetic. That I couldn't give the shards of my heart to someone else, knowing she'd never put it back together. Why inflict a broken man on someone undeserving? It's not her fault I'm damaged... it's *yours*."

With a low moan, his mouth descended and claimed hers, cutting off any hope of a reply.

ANSWERING THUNDER

*a*s Titus devoured her mouth, lightning struck, igniting an inferno that both humbled and terrified him.

The resulting firestorm herded every emotion toward him with all the galloping, thunderous peril of a runaway stagecoach. Desire in the lead, followed by possession, betrayal, hope, hunger, with the relentless lash of fury whipping the frenzy higher. Faster. Out of control.

The last time Titus had kissed this woman, she'd been Honoria Goode, a cosseted debutante who'd understood next to nothing about the wickedness of lust.

As shy and hesitant virgins, they'd swung like a wild pendulum between frenzied gropes and hot stolen kisses, to tender explorations requiring much encouragement and restraint. She'd been a tangle of insecurities and need, and he a machine of senseless desire tempered by blind, consuming love. Even still, she'd allowed him to lead her down the meandering paths of their mutual discoveries.

But now, it was Nora who held the reins in her elegant hands.

He'd been a fool to think he'd drive this interaction. That he'd control any part of it.

Nora had owned him from the moment he'd laid eyes

135

on her twenty years prior, and even though he'd captured her lips, it was *her* tongue that first staked the claim.

The depths of hell he'd endured at the loss of her, of this, were matched by an indescribable height as she licked into the seam of his lips. Withdrawing, she left the taste of sweetened tea and buttery biscuits behind.

He chased the flavor into her mouth, where their tongues met and sparred for a heated moment before he coaxed her back with a gentle sucking motion. He drank in her husky moan with the thirst born of a decade in the desert.

An answering growl vibrated from somewhere so low in his chest, he wondered if it'd originated from the abyss where his heart had resided for so long.

Lured out of the dark by the woman who'd stolen it.

If I was so easy to adore, why was I so easy to discard?

He shoved the question away as their kiss became a living thing born of need and pain and pure reclamation. He learned his temper and his lust could immolate in the same blaze, and would only be doused by *her*. He suddenly didn't care if the conflagration caught and cornered them. He would gladly burn to ash, if only to be sifted through her fingers.

Those fingers shoved into his jacket, tugging it over one shoulder in a one-handed attempt to sweep it away from him.

Her left arm remained folded in front of her as if she wore her sling, and that fact drew his head up to break the kiss.

"Help me, dammit," she panted, tugging restlessly as she lifted on her toes to reclaim his mouth.

"No," he groaned.

"I can't bloody do it myself." Her expression was a lament of lust and frustration.

As he already held her jaw in his palms, he tilted her

face up, urging her to look at him. "Your wound, Nora. We can't."

This close, her disappearing irises were the color of ripe black cherries, gleaming with striations of amber and ringed with honey. Her pupils dilated so large and round they almost swallowed everything else with a well of black, fathomless need.

"Undress," she ordered breathlessly. "*Now*."

Even as he complied, shucking his jacket and discarding it on the table, he contended, "I'll hurt you—"

"I don't care." She yanked her claws down the front of his shirt, sending more than a few of his buttons clattering against the floor and rolling in chaotic directions.

"That is because you do not understand." He caught her wrist, his thumb pressing into the pulse leaping against the thin and tender skin. He could feel the blood rushing through her veins, the electric currents leaping and arcing between them. "I'm still... furious. With *him*. With you. What is between us is not...it isn't gentle. *This* isn't—"

She yanked her wrist from his grasp before stepping in to stretch her body against his, like a cat demanding affection. Her hand lowered to shape against the cock pulsing beneath his trousers, stealing any available oxygen from his lungs.

"Be as angry as you want to be, Titus," she murmured against his ear. "Unleash it. I can bear your fury, but not your distance. I can take all of you."

With her husky permission, the rest of his control crumbled.

Her mouth was already waiting when he descended upon her with all the mercy of a wild, ravenous beast. Her body jerked as he yanked at the ties of her corset and drew it off, flinging it into the ether. He no longer knew where they were or what time it was or why they should not be doing this.

Only his body existed, and hers. They could have been Adam and Eve, every other living soul something they'd dreamed, a fabrication of their loneliness. Of their undeniable need for each other.

His lust became a ravenous, gnawing creature, hungry only to taste her. Every place she was pale and soft. Every place she was peach and delicate.

This fire between them could only be doused by a flood.

And he would make certain she was good and wet.

You'll forget them, he silently vowed. *Any other man who has had you. You'll forget them all.*

He'd always been grateful to those few women who'd been tenacious enough to entice him to enjoy the attentions they generously offered and passion they freely shared. But they'd already faded from his memory now that Nora had returned to his embrace.

His shirt only made it down to his elbows before she pushed him backward with surprising strength. He controlled his fall to the chaise, and gripped her ass as she sank with him, splitting her legs over his lap.

His hands rucked up her skirts, wading through petticoats until he found the smooth shape of her thigh, right above her knee.

This was how they would do this, the only way to protect her shoulder from discomfort or pressing up against a surface.

His body reacted with a surge of urgency and anticipation. He knew how much this woman loved to ride.

How damned good she was at it.

Beneath her thin summer chemise, the dusky tips of her breasts swayed in front of him, pebbled with arousal and need. He kissed one, then the other, breathing a hot swath through the fabric and thrilling in the delighted sounds that elicited from her throat.

Meanwhile, his hands charted a wicked path up her

thighs, stopping to tease at her garters, at the little ribbons of her drawers, plucking the one that would bare her to his touch.

They each gasped in a breath as his fingers stroked through the soft intimate hair. The heated ruffles of feminine flesh were liquid silk, molten in primitive forges.

He familiarized himself with the shape of her, marveling at the differences in their textures here. Where he was velvet skin over stone and steel, she was pliant petals and softness, yielding to his touch, to his intrusion. He tested the entrance to her body and found nothing but welcoming flesh, pulsing as if to draw him deeper inside.

"Now," she groaned, bending to press tight, needful kisses to his temples, his eyes, his cheekbones and finally, his lips. "There will be time for that," she vowed. "For all of it. But I can't live another moment without you inside me."

He could have tormented her by denying her. He wanted to. To refute her control, at the very least. To display his displeasure and his dominance. He could take his time and tease her to the edges of her own capacity.

But who was he fooling? In what world could he deny her anything?

A sigh of relief caught in his throat as he freed himself from the placket of his trousers and guided his sex toward hers.

Their eyes met, and he gloried in the connection, wanting to watch her every expression.

The intimacy seemed to overwhelm her, and she leaned in to press her temple against his, even as she lifted on trembling legs to guide the crown of his cock inside her body.

He grasped the sweet curve of her backside, stabilizing her descent with his strength as he thrust up and into her.

She gasped and wriggled a few agonizing times to ac-

KERRIGAN BYRNE

commodate him, her fingers turning to claws on his shoulders, kneading like a cat.

He was the sort of man that allowed a woman time to acquaint herself to his incursion. To kiss and cuddle and distract her from any discomfort she would feel.

But Nora didn't leave space for all of that. She made harsh, demanding, needful sounds that must have been words before they melted from her mouth.

Titus knew this language. Understood what she wanted.

He took only moments to breathe, to marvel at the magic that was sliding home. Only this moment, this need, existed. The past melted away, the future was a nebulous unknown.

She was here. Now. And all that mattered was the next hitching breath, the next caress, kiss, and thrust.

His grasp on her became covetous and unrelenting as he drove ceaselessly upwards. Titus gloried in the movements of her. The ripples of impact two people could have upon one another as they ground their flesh together until their very bones felt the force of it.

Sex for him had always been a nocturnal endeavor, and he marveled at the afternoon light gilding her pale skin, at the color decorating her chest and flaring in her cheeks. The flush of roses in her lips. The little abrasions his afternoon stubble had made against the soft skin of her mouth and cheeks.

Someday he'd leave those marks on the insides of her thighs.

The very thought brought a release threatening to gather behind his spine.

She was like a goddess above him. A Valkyrie. Battle-scarred and demanding, lifting his soul from the fray to take him to his reward.

Unable to contain his pleasure, he shifted his hand to thrum at the moist little bead where her nerves met and

140

sang. He stroked it in soft contrast to his hard thrusts, a gentle caress against the fury and frenzy.

A ragged sound ripped from her, spurring him on, faster, deeper, harder, as she arched and trembled, her strong legs keeping perfect rhythm with him. He collected her yips and sighs like a man without hope, locking them inside of his memory.

"Come for me, Nora," he ordered.

She fell forward and he caught her waist as she bit into his shoulder, just below where the collar of his open shirt rested. She shuddered and shook, her body folding in on itself as the fingers of her right hand threaded into the hair at his nape and curled into a fist.

The pain sent a lightning bolt straight to his sex as her intimate flesh pulled and released, contracting around him like a satin vise.

He didn't want this. Not yet. Not now. He wasn't ready for it to be over.

But the more he fought it, the faster and more tempestuous the storm became. Her cries of pleasure were his ultimate undoing. The articulation of her sleek body arched like a bridge over his, undulating in a rhythmic dance. For a man so moved by the mysteries of the human body, she remained an anatomical marvel. Immaculate beauty poured over a spine of steel and a heart of stone.

Or was it glass?

One he was beginning to wonder might have been just as broken as his all along.

One who'd never stopped wanting him back.

Why? The question became the metronome to his burst of increasing speed. *Why? Why? Why?*

His climax blinded him with a flash of lightning, and his resulting roars were the answering thunder as wave after wave of clenching pleasure poured from his body into hers. He was a being of both desperation and rapture, locking her hips down against his so he might allow the gentle pulses of her sex to milk the last vestiges of his own release from him.

This would never be enough, he realized as his abdominals clenched and released their last, his muscles twitching and trembling as they were finally relieved of their prison of pleasure. He would *never* be deep enough inside of her. Would never tire of holding her against him. Never want to be rid of her rose garden scent and husky, resonant voice.

Forever seemed suddenly insufficient.

And tomorrow wasn't yet decided.

He cupped the back of her head, pulling her down so her forehead could rest against his. They shared a few intimate breaths, allowing the storm to pass and the waves to still until they stood, each existed in a calm shaft of sunlight. He luxuriated in the feel of her exhales stirring at his overheated skin.

He thought he'd feel better. Sated and sleepy. Like a starving man after overindulging in a decadent meal.

He didn't.

Instead, he'd unlocked some sort of bottomless abyss that could only be filled by uninterrupted access to her.

Was he becoming like her husband? Obsessive and calculating?

No. He would never. But he certainly had decisions to make. About what kind of man he was, or would be.

"Nora," he exhaled her name from lungs still struggling to find their equilibrium. "If there's anything between us, I want it to be the truth, not the past. We should... talk."

"Don't," she sighed, stopping his lips before tracing their outline with a soft and languorous fingertip. "Let us talk tomorrow. Let tonight be about us. About this. Let me show you what you mean to me."

Her lips replaced her finger on his mouth, convincing

him instantly as he stirred inside of her. Tomorrow. They had tomorrow.

Perhaps this long dark night he'd endured without her had been a time to forge them into what they were now. To learn of loss so they could fathom abundance. To build a foundation from the failures of their youth. Perhaps... their souls and hearts were stronger and more stalwart than they might have once been, having gained the perspective of tragedy, war, hardship, and pain.

And perhaps, if the gods were kind. If they could call the past several years a recompense for any happiness they might or might not deserve, and they could find their way to forgiveness. To understanding.

And only then could he lay claim to all her days thereafter.

AN ENEMY AT THE GATE

*E*very time Nora's shoulder twinged, she couldn't help but smile. Last night, she'd thrown Titus's cautions to the wind and overexerted it, but she wasn't about to admit it to him.

She didn't regret a single moment.

Besides, the pain wasn't unbearable, and there were other aches and twinges in more intimate places that she didn't at all mind.

She'd returned her arm to the sling like an obedient patient, and now sat at the dressing table, brushing out her hair in slow, distracted strokes.

A glow that began at her center shimmered through her in breath-stealing ripples as she assessed her appearance in the mirror.

She'd been shot. A savage gangster was after her. She was a social pariah. She'd been a widow for less than a month.

And her reflection couldn't stop smiling.

She looked younger, somehow, as if making love to Titus had erased years of misery. As if sleeping in his arms had allowed her to draw from some miraculous well of recovery.

She'd lain awake for what felt like hours after, listening to him breathe. Watching his eyes flutter with dreams. He enjoyed the slumber of a man with an unburdened conscience. There was something lovely about that. Something that'd made her feel both proud and melancholy.

It didn't matter that the day had dawned grey, nor that Titus had risen before sunrise.

She could feel him close, only a few floors below. Going about his business, saving lives and alleviating pain. She'd never begrudge him that. He loved his work, and a man with such responsibilities wasn't only worthy of her regard and her admiration, but also her respect.

How long had it been since she'd respected a man?

Besides, he'd kissed her sweetly when he'd gone, smoothing a hand over her unruly morning curls, winding one around his clever finger. "I'll return for tea?" he offered in an indulgent whisper. "We have so much to discuss."

She hadn't looked forward to anything with such relish in as long as she could remember.

They could discuss the past, of course. And then... turn their eyes to the future.

Was this hope? This glow in her chest? This soft, bubbling effervescence that made her feel as if her blood were rendered of champagne. It'd been so long since she'd felt anything of the kind, she couldn't exactly place a name on it.

The only thing she knew for certain: Titus was the cause. He was the cure to her ills and the balm to her soul.

He had the heart of a saint, the body of a god, and the appetite of a libertine.

William had grown soft and bloated in their years together, his hair thin and his middle thick. His teeth yellowed by vice and lack of consistent hygienic practices. Everything about him, from his breath to the sound of his voice, used to offend her.

Perhaps she might have felt differently had she loved him... if he'd been worthy of her regard in any respect.

Titus was as different from him as night was from day. Age had only improved upon what youth had rendered. Muscles developed through labor as a lad were kept taut with strength from training at the club with some of his compatriots from the army.

Even his scent enticed her, so sharp and clean, mixed with the cedar of his wardrobe and the spice of his after-shave. His voice had crooned wicked things into her ears with the resonance and reverence of cathedral bells, vi-brating to the very soul of her.

After the tumult of their first encounter, their love-making had become more leisurely and deliberate, enough to where they were able to rediscover each other with inexhaustible delight.

They'd had to be creative with her shoulder, finding positions that didn't jostle her too terribly, nor could she bear weight.

Nora clamped her lips together as she remembered the way he'd gently rolled her on her side, curling his lithe, strong body against her back and lifting her leg in the air to enter her from behind.

She'd allowed herself to luxuriate in all the sensations of him. The tickle of the hair on his thighs against her backside. The corrugations of his ribs as he'd rolled and contracted.

And his clever, lovely fingers as they—

A knock sounded at the door, distracting her from her salacious reverie. Likely Felicity come to keep her com-pany. She stood, abandoning her brush to the table, and swept down the hall, adjusting her sling as she went.

Her excitement bubbled over even before she was able to reach the door. "Felicity, darling, you'll never guess what—"

The Baron Cresthaven, her father, stood where she'd

expected to find her sister, his hands locked behind his back in his requisite regimental posture.

Though it had been only weeks since she'd seen him, he seemed older, somehow. Even though he still towered over her, he might have lost a bit of height. His beard seemed threaded with more grey and silver, and the lines at his eyes and mouth grooved deeper into his skin.

"Papa," she croaked through her surprise. She'd lived with the man for the first twenty years of her life, had seen him often thereafter, and she could still never tell if his features were indignant, or just arranged thusly.

"Honoria," he greeted with a bland sort of insouciance. As if he were disappointed to find her there, even though she could be the only person he'd come to see.

She pulled the door open wider, stepping aside. "Won't you come in?"

He walked through the entryway to Titus's private apartments, and she became immediately distraught and defensive. He was an interloper here. A tremulous anxiety caused her to feel slightly ill, his presence covering her previous good cheer like a cold, damp blanket made of scratchy wool.

Still, a little seed of hope bloomed within her. Perhaps it was finally deemed safe enough for him to visit. Or he'd news from home.

Was it too much to hope he pitied her? That he worried for her wellbeing after all that'd transpired...

She'd almost lost her life, his firstborn. Did that mean something to him?

Trailing him as he strode down the hall and into the great room arranged to make the most of the splendid views of the city, she asked, "Does Doctor Conleith know you've come? Would you like me to ring for some tea?"

"No, I won't be staying long." He blinked over at the tasteful furnishings, the damask drapes, the expensive sconces and bric-a-brac. She hated that she held her breath to hear what verdict he might pass.

He said nothing as he paused at the high-backed chair Titus favored, and put his hand on the crest, posing like a royal in a painting. He made a quick assessment of her unbound hair and the frothy gown that reminded her of the purple pansies in their gardens. "You're not wearing widow's black, Honoria."

Any hope for paternal concern evaporated like the morning fog from the Thames when sliced by shafts of sunlight through the buildings. "You don't actually expect me to mourn William, Papa; he was a murderer and a monster."

"I know very well what he was. He used my shipping company to smuggle for a gangster, if you'll remember." He exclaimed this as if it were William's worst sin of the lot, before his eyes narrowed upon her. "Still, tradition dictates you wear black. It is imperative that you're seen doing everything properly."

Deflating, she gestured to the arm bound to her body. "I'm not *seen* doing anything at all, Father. That's rather the point of being in hiding. I see no one but my sisters, Nurse Higgins, and Doctor Conleith."

"Yes... Conleith." He gave their lush surroundings another thorough inspection, as if looking for something to condemn them. To Nora's smug relief, their surroundings were every bit as fine as the furniture at Cresthaven. The rooms even larger and the amenities more tasteful and modern.

Her mother often pointed out to her father that they could relocate to some of the grander and newer houses being built in Belgravia and beyond, but Clarence Goode stubbornly held on to their Mayfair square, the one where the names were ancient and the titles as archaic as the homes.

Such things mattered more to him than anything,

after money, of course. Tradition, position, reputation, followed by zealotry disguised as faith.

What an empty and terrible way to live. It was such a shame she could only come to that conclusion after the worst had happened. After she'd lost everything that *he* held dear. Her position in society, her reputation.

But what she'd found with Titus was so much more precious than that.

Passion, acceptance, a sense of wholeness, hope, and wonder. And—someday—forgiveness?

Dare she hope...love.

"That boy is taking a great risk keeping you here," her father remarked.

"Morley doesn't think so. Since Mr. Sauvageau doesn't seem to know I'm here—"

He pinned her with his most imperious glare. "I'm not referring to the gangsters, Honoria, but everyone else. Everyone who matters. Though your circumstances are *greatly* diminished and Conleith's have exponentially elevated, so much about the impossibility of your situation remains unchanged."

"*Doctor* Conleith," she dared to correct him, wanting her father to give Titus his due. "And I don't understand—"

"Of course you don't," he snorted. "*Doctor* Conleith has both made and spent an impressive and astonishing fortune on a bevy of new surgical schemes, or so I've gathered."

"I know this already—"

"He's still nobody, Honoria. He is nothing without his reputation as a surgeon and a man. He has no title to protect him, no lands to rely upon for income. His entire future is built upon the skill in his hands and the trust of his wealthy patients and patrons here."

The weight of all that was pressing upon Titus's shoulders became a heavy lead stone in her gut. Because she knew what her father's next words would be. And the truth they contained threatened to extinguish the tiny flame of hope with which she'd awoken, and plunge her into a pit of despair.

"A relationship with you could taint him. You realize that, don't you? You could ruin the success of any of his future endeavors. That's how far and completely you have fallen."

Her legs gave way as her father yanked the rug out from under them, and she landed on the velvet chair behind her.

Hard.

Cresthaven reached into the pocket of the mahogany vest that stretched over his impressive paunch and retrieved his watch to check the time.

As if he had somewhere more important to be.

"Your mother and I have discovered a way out of this debacle you've found yourself in."

At that, her temper flared. "I didn't *find* myself anywhere, Father. My husband tried to murder me. This was no fault of mine."

He waved his hand in front of his face, as if dispelling an unpleasant scent or swatting away a fly.

"This past Sunday, I was approached by the Duke of Bellingham. Apparently, his second son, Mark, is in need of a wife, and they're willing to take you on after the appropriate period of mourning. You'll be married next summer in Devon, so... enjoy this little rendezvous while you can."

"Take me on?" she echoed, aghast. "You're mad if you think I'll be impressed upon to marry again, Father; I barely *survived* the last one!"

He stepped forward, his threatening manner causing her to flinch away. Her father hadn't been a heavy-handed parent, but he'd slapped them a few times if they'd provoked him enough.

"Think of someone other than yourself for once, Honoria," he blustered, his chins vibrating with the violence of his unchecked disdain. "Mercy and Felicity are being treated abominably, shunned from society, and openly mocked. Their chances at decent marriages are effectively nil. Your mother is possibly on her deathbed with nervous conniptions, her heart growing weaker by the day. I've had to instruct the staff to hide the papers and the cordial from her. Business like mine is built on reputation, you daft girl. What do you think will happen to our wealth if our name is in tatters? You are not the only one who has suffered, but you're the only one who can reclaim some semblance of our family's honor in the wake of this disaster."

Suddenly dizzy, Nora pressed her hand to her forehead, unable to tell if she were feverish, or if her hands were abnormally cold.

She should have known. She was aware of what the *ton* did to those who fell out of favor. Nothing that her father had imparted should have been news to her.

But her sisters had never let on their distress, hadn't mentioned her mother's condition. She'd been more than happy to stay cossetted in this tower like a damaged princess, forgetting that she wasn't the only person in danger. That the ripples of her husband's actions would affect the innocent, and that she had some responsibility to amend that.

She'd never really considered that *she* could become Titus's ruin. Because he was such a strong and stalwart man. Capable and gifted and ruthless and resilient, she no more assumed she could cause him harm than a butterfly could destroy a lion.

But it was so much worse than that.

She could ruin him with her affection.

Again.

Was it some sort of curse? To have him for moments

of bliss, only to have to choose between him and honor? Or to make him chose between her and ruination?

"Why would a Duke invite someone like me into his family?" she asked, kneading at her temple.

Her father's gaze darted away, sliding a dagger of unease into her ribs. "He's a victim of his own scandal. Mark was kept from prison only by the hand of his father, the Duke. He's an invert, so he's being forced to go into the church... being a vicar's wife will do you some good, I think."

"An invert." She dropped her hand in surprise. "You mean, he prefers the romantic company of...men?"

"Evidently fell in love with some French actor. There are photographs." Her father shuddered. "He's reported to be nothing like William, thank God. A gentle sort of fellow, studious and dull."

Honoria instantly felt a tug of pity for Mark.

If not for Titus, such an arrangement might suit her quite well. A kind man, one who wouldn't make sexual demands of her. A quiet life in a country vicarage. She didn't so much mind the idea of men being lovers, couldn't understand why it was considered such a sin to begin with.

A click from down the hall toward the entry told her the door had been opened and shut. The sound preceded Titus's footsteps down the hall. She knew the cadence of his confident stride, and she stood suddenly. Her heart at once surged to her throat, only to take a nosedive into the pit of her belly.

This was impossible. No matter what she did, she hurt him.

If she ended it, she sliced through the tenuous bond they'd only just forged. She broke his heart again, just when he'd begun to open it.

If she stayed... she might cost him everything. His patients and his patrons. His entire life's work. Everyone she loved would suffer for that love. She was like a fragmented bomb, laying waste to all who dared to stand in her immediate vicinity.

Her father, apparently, hadn't marked Titus's approach. "I suppose you and Mark will both have to learn to be discreet with your lovers. But perhaps he'll allow you to keep your doctor on the line. Then, you won't have to cease being a whore."

Titus rounded the corner, looking every bit the gentleman doctor. Hair tidy, jaw clean-shaven, his expensive grey vest buttoned over a shirt rolled up to the elbows.

Except...

He didn't spare Nora half a glance before he marched up to the Baron, his features a black mask of wrath and retribution as he used his only slightly superior height to look down his nose.

"It is part of my personal creed to do no harm," he said in a voice measured only with darkness. "But in your case, I'm willing to make an exception."

His fist drove into her father's face with all the force of a locomotive, knocking the imposing man over.

Nora rushed forward. Though her father had fallen to his hip, he was still sitting up, holding one hand over his nose. Blood leaked through his fingers as he let loose a string of curses he could have only picked up at the docks.

Titus shook out his hand a few times, testing the mobility of his fingers before glaring down at the man he'd put on the ground.

Even though he looked as though he'd like to murder her father, he reached into his pocket and extracted a handkerchief, dangling it in the Baron's line of sight.

Lord, but he was an endlessly decent man.

Her father hesitated for a moment, but then took the offering and shoved it beneath his nose with a pained groan. "In your case, I suppose I deserved that," he said, his voice almost comically nasal and muffled by the handkerchief.

"What is *deserved* is an apology to your *daughter*." Titus looked like an avenging angel, ready to go to battle, wielding his righteous indignation. "It is your fault she is in danger. All of this was caused by the man you selected for her. Tell me, Cresthaven, did you know the Viscount was mad before pledging her to him?"

Dammit, she just fell in love with him again.

"You can stay out of this." Her father managed to be imposing, even as he leaned his head back to stem the flow of blood from his nose. "Even now, she's as far above you as the stars are above the treetops."

"You don't think I always knew that?" Titus gestured to her, keeping his palm up as an invitation for her to take his hand.

Instinctively Nora reached for him, but then she hesitated. All the words her father said barraged her conscience like a thousand pricks from a thousand daggers.

You will ruin him. He will hate you for it.

Not as much as you'll hate yourself.

"Honoria," her father warned. "If you stay, this place will be leveled to rubble at *your* feet."

Titus loomed over him, his fist tightening once again. "Don't you dare threaten me or this institution."

"I'm not, lad. I'm simply telling you the truth."

"I'm no lad, you sanctimonious bastard. I'm a doctor, and a soldier, and a scientist. I deserve—"

"You deserve to keep what you've built and to retain the respect you've earned."

Both Titus and Nora stood there for a moment, jaws loose as they stared at the man struggling not to bleed onto the carpet.

Had he just paid Titus a compliment?

The Baron pinched the bridge of his nose with a wince, but he was a hard man, not unused to a swinging fist at the docks in his younger days. "I already told Honoria, an alliance with her could ruin everything for you. Her reputation is in tatters, man."

"My associates aren't as easily frightened off by a little scandal as yours are," Titus remonstrated.

"We both know that's not true."

Titus's eyes flicked away from Nora's questioning look, and with that, her decision was made.

And her heart was shattered.

The Baron only spoke the truth. Her love was the kiss of death, and Titus knew it.

Woodenly, she went to her father and bent to help him up with her one good hand.

"Nora. Don't." Titus reached down and lifted the Baron easily, stabilizing him on his feet before turning to her. "I don't care about all that, I never have. We can find a way to..."

"It's impossible," she murmured.

"No, it isn't. Listen to me—"

"You don't know what you're up against," her father said, checking the handkerchief to see if he'd stopped bleeding. "Her sisters are ostracized and persecuted. The press hound us at every turn, making it damned near impossible to leave the house. They camped out at the offices of my company. Two clerks quit. Poor Felicity had a tomato thrown at her the other day by one of the sisters of your dead prostitutes, Honoria. Can you imagine what that did to the bashful pigeon? She almost came undone."

Nora closed her eyes, pierced by unrelenting shame. *Her sweet sister...how could she bear it?*

She'd been a fool to hope. Last night had been nothing but a fantasy, and now her father had torn that fiction asunder with harsh but pertinent realities.

Could he not have waited? One more day. One more night?

Titus shook his head over and over, patently rejecting

what she was about to do. "I can help your sisters, Nora. I have powerful allies. We can change the narrative, can influence the press. I've seen it done numerous times."

"We can change the narrative, but we can't change the truth," she said, her words sounding droll and dead, even to her. "Not about me."

Titus's teeth clacked shut, and he looked as if she'd slapped him.

True to her form, instead of pulling back at the sight of his pain, she forged ahead, ready to rip herself out of his heart once and for all. "It doesn't change that William killed an Earl. That my sisters are suffering the consequences of my actions because I besmirched myself with other men. And that you will suffer, too."

He lunged forward, gripping her hands in his. "I'll survive it, Nora. I've survived worse than—"

Her father scoffed. "You can't know that, Doctor. I've seen many a businessman obliterated by reputation—"

"You've made your bloody point, Cresthaven. I advise you to not interject into this conversation again." A finger jabbed in her father's direction was all it took to press the Baron's lips together, his mottled skin blanching a little.

Despite her astonishment at her father's naked fear, Nora persisted. "I refuse to be something you survive, Titus."

"That's not what I—"

"I've made my decision." She pulled her hands from his warm grip, already grieving. Mourning. Lamenting his loss. She felt shriveled and bleak, hollowed out by pain. To walk out of here would age her another decade at least.

But she'd do it. For him.

His face hardened. His eyes becoming chips of ore, molten in the flames of his temper. "You. Decided," he bit out. "Because that's what you do, isn't it? You make the decision and I have to abide by it."

"Yes," she answered sedately.

"I don't get a say. I don't get a choice. You just run away without trusting that I might know better than him. That we might form a solution together."

"I really am sorry," she said, her throat threatening to close over the pain. She wished it would, that she could stop her breath right here and sink into oblivion. Sorry didn't begin to touch the desperate regret threatening to pull her under. "It's hopeless, Titus. I was always going to damage you one way or the other. And this is bigger than you or me. This is Mercy and Felicity. My parents. Your patients. The families devastated by both my choices and William's. If there were any other way without damaging those I love..."

He held his hand up to silence her, turning his face to the side as if he couldn't bear the sight of her. Already his knuckles were swelling, and she wanted nothing more than to kiss them. His perfect, brilliant surgeon's hands.

Ones that had saved her life twice now.

Perhaps it would have been better if he hadn't, if he'd let fate have its way with her so he wouldn't feel so tethered.

So she wouldn't feel this agony.

Perhaps they were always meant to belong to something—someone—else. She to her family's honor. He to his craft.

"You do what you have to, Nora," he said, his features cast from granite. "But don't for one *minute* think that you're protecting me. Because I'd have burned this entire place to the ground if it meant having a life with you in it."

He left in measured strides. Driven away a second time.

"That's just it," she whispered. "I'd *never* ask you to."

THE EVENING OF

*A*fter a week of exhausting himself with punishing amounts of work, Titus had recently discovered drinking as a simpler anesthetic than constant distraction.

After his second brown ale, the tension in his bones loosened, and the aches abated. After two or three subsequent glasses of whiskey—or gin, if he were desperate enough—he could almost convince himself that he didn't miss her.

Almost.

Her loss had always been an emptiness he couldn't seem to fill, but this time was especially cruel.

Because he couldn't even stay angry with her.

She'd thrown herself on a sword, becoming a martyr to misery out of some misguided sense of honor.

Perhaps misguided wasn't the word… she'd made some salient points, after all. Fate, it seemed, wanted them to choose between their happiness.

Or the lives of others.

But he was a scientist, goddammit. He was a man who —when presented with a conundrum—reveled in the solving of it. There had to be a way, and if she wasn't willing to find it, he would.

Perhaps at the bottom of his glass.

"Do you want another one, Morley?" he asked, raising his hand to the barkeep at the Hatchet and Crown. War veterans and officers often took their respite at this mahogany bar, therefore a man with a bleak expression and desire for solitude could find a place to drink unmolested. Men here often wallowed in their loneliness together.

As the chief inspector was a fair-skinned man, his cheeks now glowed with warmth as he pushed his glass away and fought to contain a belch. "I've had quite enough, which is still two fewer than you. I'll have to pour you into a hackney."

"I'll get him back home." Dorian yawned from where he perched on Titus's other side, and drained his stout. "I've business in that part of town anyway."

"Do I want to know what sort of business?" Morley goaded.

"You probably already do, you meddling cur." Dorian's eye patch hid his expression until he turned to flash a taunting smile at them both.

"He said he deserved it," Titus told the inside of his glass, puzzling over the same conversation for two weeks now. "What did he mean?"

"Who?" Morley and Dorian asked at the same time.

"Nora's father." Titus wondered when he'd begun to slur. He didn't even feel that inebriated. "What did the Baron mean when he said he deserved a punch from me? Why would he say that? Because he put me on the streets? What man wouldn't for deflowering his daughter?"

"Enough of this." Morley relieved him of his glass, which still had another two hefty swallows. "It's only making you maudlin. You'll be bound to the bottle if you keep it up."

Reflexively, Titus plucked the glass back and downed it in one burning gulp, before slamming the glass onto the bar with a resounding noise. "One does well to treat an outside wound with alcohol," he contended. "But it is also an effective treatment for internal injuries."

"Sound science." Dorian shrugged into his coat.

"Yes," Titus heartily agreed. "The soundest of hypothessissiess. Hupothesi? Hypotenuse."

Suddenly his stomach lurched, and he tried to remember if he'd eaten since breakfast. He'd no appetite lately. No vigor. Everything tasted flat and beige.

"Come on, man." Dorian hauled him to his feet. "Let's get you home to bed."

"I don't sleep in my bed. It smells like roses."

He missed the glance his compatriots shared because he felt a perfectly good brood coming upon him.

"*I'm*—I should have stopped her." He swayed, looking for his hat before Morley shoved the thing into his hands. "I should have just trussed her up and thrown her in my carriage and run away to Italy. But who does that kind of thing?"

"Only the best of men," Dorian said cheekily. "So, I cannot argue the point."

Morley reached in his pockets and left a generous several coins on the bar. "Prudence says Lady Woodhaven is as bereft as you are. She hasn't accepted any kind of proposal. Not officially. There's still time to fight for her, you know."

His still, cold heart began to beat at the prospect, thrumming and stalling as if it'd forgotten how. "I'd fight the entire world for her... if she'd let me."

A youngish man with an air of danger and an overconfident swagger came toward them. Titus braced for trouble, but the lad merely handed a folded note to Blackwell, tipped his hat at the gratuity he received, and melted back into the London night.

Dorian opened the note and read quickly, his lips compressing into a tight line.

"What is it?" Morley asked, suddenly alert.

"It would seem we're going to Sheerness," he said.

"But that's...hours downriver," Titus protested, stumbling out onto cobbles shining in the pallid gaslight from a recent rain.

"Which is fortunate for you, because you'll need to sober up on the way." Dorian whistled and motioned to where his carriage waited idly a block down. "It would seem your errant lady love has hired an entire handful of personal safety guards to conduct her and her two sisters there tonight rather than wait for the train. Can you imagine why?"

Titus's heart kicked up plenty now, his hands and feet blanching cold while his ears burned, and his lungs tightened. "A town at the mouth of the Thames? I can't begin to guess—"

He broke away, as logic threaded through his whisky-soaked thoughts. He knew her. Even though they'd spent so much of their lives apart. He still knew her. Knew what drove her decisions and desires. She wanted to make amends. To free her sisters from her tainted reputation, possibly by untainting it.

"What is in Sheerness?" he demanded.

Dorian shrugged, searching his near perfect memory. "Oh, a few hotels, an estuary, a fishing and shipping port, mostly."

"Shipping, you say?" Morley clipped, cutting a look across to Titus as Dorian's carriage pulled to the curb. "If they're after what I think they are, let's hope they took a bloody army with them, because they're going to need it."

"Why do you say that?" Titus asked. "I thought she was no longer being followed."

The Chief Inspector glanced through the darkened streets as if searching for a tail. "If Blackwell knows where she's gone, there's a good chance Sauvageau does, as well. The messenger network in this city might be fast and reliable, but serves any master with coin. They know no such thing as loyalty."

Blackwell nodded grimly as he called the footman down from his carriage. "Tell Farah I'll be home in the morning... we have wild beasts to hunt tonight."

THAT AFTERNOON OF

Though her shoulder was healing nicely, the rest of Nora remained one jagged, bleeding wound. And only one doctor in the world could hope to stitch her back together.

She'd eaten more crow in the past couple of weeks than she'd prepared to, and suffered a multitude of indignities. The worst of which was clearing what was left of her things from the home that would be occupied by Adrian McKendrick, the new Viscount Woodhaven.

It wasn't that she was at all attached to the home she'd shared with William. Merely that she was convinced that by the time she married the son of a duke, she'd not have a shred of dignity to offer anyone.

It was worth it, she kept reminding herself. To once again secure Titus's future, along with—

A loud crash from below broke her reverie, and she called down the stairs to where Mercy and Felicity argued in the parlor. "Is everything all right?"

"It's splendid!" Mercy sang back. "Nothing amiss down here!"

"A vase tipped." Felicity emerged from the parlor to the hall where Nora could see her from the second floor. She was holding two larger shards of pottery and wearing a chagrined expression. "We were packing the library when a spirited debate over the superiority of romances or mysteries turned into a fencing match with the fireplace implements. Mercy cut her hand."

"Don't be cross!" Mercy's plea sounded more like a command, though she still hid out of view.

"I'll be right down." Nora checked out the window for the guards her father had hired to stand sentinel against either gangsters or reporters. She wondered if any of them knew a wit about doctoring wounds.

They stood on the walk, looking much too brutish and conspicuous for such a quiet square.

She hurried to fetch a kit of bandages and iodine from the washroom and flew downstairs to the parlor.

Felicity swept up the vase and Mercy was sitting like a child about to be scolded, her fist curled around a handkerchief.

"I'm not cross, it's only a vase," Nora said with a fond smile, holding her hand out. "Where are you hurt?"

"It's a trifle." Mercy unclenched her hand and pulled back a handkerchief, revealing a cut on her palm that still welled with blood. "When the vase fell, I lunged for it and, clumsy dolt that I am, I fell right on top of it."

"It's bleeding *so* much," Felicity said with a delicate, dyspeptic burp. "I can't look, or I'll be sick. Or faint."

"It appears worse than it is." Mercy inspected it. "So superficial, I can't imagine it'll even need stitches."

"A small mercy that," Nora murmured, dabbing a ball of cotton with the iodine and pressing it gently to the cut.

"Why?" Mercy queried. "Because the closest clinic happens to be Dr. Conleith's surgery?" She waggled expressive brows, her wide, mischievous mouth twisting in a suggestive grin. "I *still* can't believe he broke father's nose."

"I'd have given anything to have seen it," Felicity sighed.

At that, Nora shoved a bandage into Mercy's wounded hand, and promptly burst into tears.

Her sisters instantly bracketed her like two clucking bookends, their hands fluttering on her back and her arm like anxious butterflies unsure of where to land.

Nora wrestled with her runaway emotion, doing her best to rein it back in, but each bawl seemed more gasping than the last, until every breath dragged through hiccupping sobs.

Felicity crooned to her, rubbing little comforting circles against her spine as Mercy affixed a one-handed makeshift bandage on her own palm.

"You love Titus, don't you?" Felicity sighed, resting her chin on Nora's uninjured shoulder.

Nora shook her head, accepting the handkerchief Felicity handed her, and dabbing at her eyes and nose. "Don't mark this, either of you. It's been a trying time and I'm…it doesn't matter."

She took in a deep, painful breath and swallowed the ocean of tears threatening to sweep her into the tide. "What matters is that next year I'll be married to a Duke's son, Titus will be the toast of the elite scientific and surgical community, and you… you'll be the belles of the season with dowries the size of which London has not yet seen, if Father is to be believed." She smoothed the skirt of her black gown and took in several calming breaths. "There's still hope," she reminded herself.

Felicity pulled her hands back as if she were made of burning rubbish. "Hope for what?"

"For you both. For good marriages."

The twins looked quizzically at her, and then each other, before they astonished her by bursting into peals of unladylike guffaws.

"What on *earth* makes you think we want to be married?" Mercy ended a chortle with an accidental snort, which sent them both into another tumult of amusement.

Felicity wiped tears from the corner of her eyes. "I believe the idioms, *not if the entire world depended on it*, and *never in a million years* have been batted around."

Nora stared at them as if they were each two heads of a hydra. "But...you're being bullied terribly. Shunned from society. Not invited to participate in the season."

"And?" Mercy shrugged. "That leaves us time to attend lectures and meetings, and it's ever so much easier on Felicity that she doesn't have to talk to men. Or look at them. Let alone marry one, can you imagine?"

Felicity sobered at this a little, but seemed sincere when she said, "We've decided all we need is each other's company. *No* husbands. Ever."

Nora shook her head, unable to comprehend. "But... without husbands how will you afford to live?"

Mercy shrugged. "Well, Father's on the hook for our upkeep indefinitely."

Alarmed, Nora grasped her uninjured hand and forced Mercy to meet her gaze. "Father is unforgiving if you defy him like this. He'll throw you to the wolves if you're of no use to him; believe me when I tell you that."

Mercy stood, pulling her hand from Nora's frantic grasp, her eyes blazing with a sapphire zeal. "We'll become governesses then, or seamstresses. Companions or stuffy old librarians. But I'll see a cold day in hell before I see myself in a church as a bride."

Felicity put her hand on Nora's knee. "Is that why you came back, Nora? To fix our reputations?"

Choking on another sob, Nora clapped a hand over her mouth.

Mercy sighed and regained her seat at Nora's side, her curls spilling over her riotous magenta bodice. This time, she seized Nora's hand, and then thought better of it, gripping her beneath the chin like a recalcitrant child. "Stop it," she ordered with much more confidence and command than her tender years should have afforded

her. "You stop martyring yourself for us or for anyone else. I'll not have it. Neither of us gives a fig if the house of Goode is sullied, and—regardless of what Father says— it's certainly no fault of yours."

"Go be happy, Nora. Please," Felicity admonished. "We'll be all right. We'll be better than that. The worst has already happened, the damage has been done. Not by you but your terrible husband."

Mercy released her so she could look over to Felicity, an identical face, if softer and more earnest. "You needn't endure any longer. You never should have done. Father is dreaming if he thinks this marriage will save everything. But one thing isn't a dream... Titus Conleith loves you. He has always loved you. And you love him, I think."

Nora shook her head, her heart bursting with love for her sisters and pain for her loss.

Of course she loved Titus. All she'd ever done was because she'd loved him.

"He hates me now, I'm certain of it," she sniffled, wiping away tears that refused to stop falling. "I left with Father when he all but begged me not to. I betrayed him again."

Felicity took off her spectacles and rubbed some fog away on her sleeve before replacing them. "According to the novels I read, if his feelings for you are powerful in either direction... that means there's hope for a happy ending yet."

"I don't know if he'll ever trust me," she lamented. "I've been so unspeakably cruel."

Mercy perked up. "What *do* they do in your novels, Felicity, when it seems all hope is lost?"

Nora plucked at a stray thread in the handkerchief. "It doesn't matter, it never ends well for the villain."

Felicity shook her head forcefully. "No, you're not the villain. You're the hero, and Titus—regardless of his apparent virility and... impressive musculature—is the heroine."

Nora looked at her askance. "How do you figure?"

"Well, you've the reputation of a rake, I gather." Felicity blushed as she said this, pressing a hand to her cheek. "And have wounds from a dark and painful past."

Mercy held her finger up to mark an idea. "You were shot at least once and stalked by diabolical fiends of the underworld."

"That's right!" agreed Felicity. "That makes you the dashing—if somewhat imperfect—hero."

Even Nora couldn't fight the tug of a smile at their antics. Bless the souls of bookworms everywhere. "So, what does the hero do to win back his heroine?"

Felicity tapped her chin. "Usually a grand gesture of some kind. The hero realizes he was utterly wrong and dreadful—sorry Nora—and he does something to make himself ridiculous for his heroine. Or he fixes all her problems and restores her honor and good name. He saves her from the villain—"

"Titus doesn't need saving from anyone except for me... that hasn't changed."

"Tosh," Mercy shoved that idea aside with a wave of her glove. "I'm sure he needs *something*; we only have to figure out what that is. What is the conflict? What would keep you two apart?"

Nora cast about for ideas, feeling too cynical to be this idealistic. And yet...

"I suppose Titus needs funding to expand his new clinics, and for that he needs financiers, investors, and wealthy patrons to his surgery. He wants to open one in every borough, so even the poor can be treated in time without having to solely rely on the underfunded and overwhelmed city hospitals."

"So, it's just a question of money." Mercy shrugged as if that were no insurpable impediment. "If you can figure out how to replace what he might lose through... well through scandalous association with a benighted—if beautiful—widow, then what's to keep you from being together?"

Nora stood, suddenly agitated by a relentless pinprick of hope in a dark abysmal sky. "It's not *merely* money, it's everything. I'm still possibly a mark for this Sauvageau person because William is haunting me with misfortune from beyond the grave."

"If only we could find that gold William took," Felicity mused. "Surely that would be enough to finance any manner of medical marvels."

Nora put a hand to her forehead and squeezed, hoping to bring forward any idea, any helpful memory. "Before he died, William was looking in shipping containers at the Southwark warehouse because it is largely unused in Father's business. The rest of the London warehouses were subsequently searched by Morley."

"What about the one in Sheerness?"

Nora turned to Mercy very slowly, her blood suddenly pulsing through her. "Say that again."

Mercy's eyes shifted restlessly or—one could say—guiltily. "Well one time, when Prudence and I were snooping through Papa's papers, I thought... I would like to figure out just how rich Father is."

"And?" Nora breathed.

"He's obscenely affluent. Perhaps wealthier than the Queen."

Felicity frowned. "I knew we were rich, but to listen to Father go on, it's as if we're on the verge of ruin at all times."

"The warehouse, Mercy," Nora redirected the conversation back to the salient topic, doing her level best not to snipe at her sisters.

"Oh, well, Father has a few warehouses closer to the mouth of the Thames. According to the papers I found, they've been for sale for months, but the rafters are rotting, so no one's been interested. He's planning on razing and liquidating the property." She put her fists on her hips. "Did you know, he has estate holdings all over, in the strangest of places. Houses we never knew existed?"

This seemed to increase Felicity's distress. "What does he do with them?"

"Who is to say?"

Nora put a hand to her heart, just below the still-healing wound that now ached when she became so tense. "It could be there," she whispered. "Morley has no jurisdiction in Sheerness."

"Should we send for him?" Felicity suggested. "For safety's sake, if nothing else."

"No, you ninny," Mercy stood as well and began to pace as she considered. "If we invite the police, they'll confiscate the gold."

"The gold has been stolen from someone..." Nora reasoned. "Even if we find it, it's not ours."

"We'd be taking from smugglers to finance medical care for the poor," Mercy remonstrated. "We're essentially Robin Hood."

Nora couldn't believe she was about to do this. "I'm not getting you two involved. You need to return home at once."

"Oh, no you don't!" Mercy wagged her finger, then winced as she jostled her wounded hand. "You're not leaving us out of this adventure. I've been reading about quests for illicit treasure my entire life and I'm finally able to go on one!"

"I do think we should hire more security...and probably shouldn't leave until after dark."

"Excellent!" Mercy swept to the front door. "I'll just ask our entourage if they have any dangerous-looking friends."

DAWN

$\mathcal{T}$itus was stone-cold sober by the time he reached Sheerness.

As they careened through the sleepy port town, dawn licked the eastern sky with silver. Clouds built a swirling mass in the distance, pregnant with an approaching storm. The ocean ebbed and surged in a murky maelstrom, as a swarming flock of dark birds waved and shifted like an ominous flag above.

When the carriage clattered up to the dilapidated warehouse at #12 Seaworthy Street—the address on Dorian's note—Titus leapt from the carriage before it even had a chance to slow down. Clutching his medical bag in one hand and a wicked iron-tipped club in the other, he realized he was more ready to use the unfamiliar weapon than the typical tools.

After suffering through the past couple of weeks, he was ready to break something.

Or someone.

The warehouse stood gaunt and bleak, hunkering alone over a vacant dock. It was as if the tightly clustered shipyard businesses to the south and north had turned their backs, leaving it to rot abandoned and alone.

Dim light flickered from a window in the corner

facing the water. Along one dark alley, two passenger carriages and a cart used for hauling freight were hitched to sleepy horses. Their breaths curled from their nostrils into the chill of the morning, and Titus could almost hear the sound, so complete was the eerie silence.

Still as death.

What if they were too late?

Dread and fury threatened to overwhelm him, tunneling his vision with shades of crimson. *Nora.* His heart tattooed the syllables of her name into his ribs.

"Wait, dammit," Morley growled as his and Dorian's boots hit the ground behind Titus. "We don't know what is awaiting us in there."

"She's in there. That's all I need to know." Even as he said it, he paced at the door, desperately listening for signs of life. He looked behind him to see Morley hang a rifle over his shoulder.

"That woman is banned from entering warehouses for the rest of her natural life," the Chief Inspector muttered with no small amount of exasperation.

"Upon that, you can rely," Titus vowed, grappling back both wrath and worry in an effort to summon the strength to discover whatever horror might await them inside. "Where is the security they hired?"

"I was wondering that myself." Blackwell, a man fond of wearing long jackets even in the summer, had any number of weapons hidden on him at any given time. Whether he currently palmed a knife or a pistol remained to be seen. "Tell me you have a firearm in that bag, Doctor."

"Trust me," Titus said darkly. "I've instruments in here that would cause you nightmares."

"Good. Let us hope we don't need them."

"There's nowhere to climb," Morley grumbled, his head tilted back to survey the drooping, dangerously sloped roof of the structure. "And no windows low enough to get to."

"The front door it is, then." Titus lifted his boot and kicked the door. The latch shattered and wood splintered as the thing exploded inward on rusted hinges.

They advanced into the gloom of the warehouse, Titus at their head, using the darkness on the street side to their advantage.

What he saw confounded him enough to freeze his feet to the floor.

The warehouse was an empty void of packed earth and mold. The air stirred with a sharp bite of pitch. Tired beams held aloft sagging rafters and a second-floor walkway was missing more boards than it boasted. A handful of shipping crates clustered at the top of a ramp that led out to the water, if freight wanted to be loaded onto smaller crafts.

A lone lantern perched on a crate and haloed three slim women, who stood abreast on the platform behind an open chest. Clad in dark colors as they were, the Goode sisters might have been hovering over a child's coffin rather than a gleaming fortune.

Titus's heart came alive at the sight of Nora, standing between her fair sisters like a midnight angel. He devoured her with his gaze, his vision blurred with exhaustion and unbridled emotion.

He released her name on a relieved breath, breaking into a jog toward her.

She shook her head, the warning in her wide eyes piercing him with caution the moment before a lone man melted from the shadows beneath the landing.

He maneuvered in front of the women and the chest with the deceptively sleek insouciance of a snake. But Titus could see that this serpent was coiled, ready to strike at the slightest provocation. He was neither bulky nor slight, tall nor short. Though his proportions were hidden beneath, an exquisitely tailored blue suit suggested at imposing strength and ideal ratios. Dark hair gleamed almost blue in the lantern light, and a diamond winked from one ear.

Titus's fist curled around his club in readiness. Though the man appeared unarmed and unaccompanied, he knew a predator when he saw one.

This particular predator had the raw-boned, sharp-jawed elegance that would have suited the archangel for which he was named.

Raphael Sauvageau.

"The Black Heart of Ben More." The gangster bowed at the waist, adopting a smile that was dangerously close to a sneer. "It is an incomparable honor. I have been an ardent pupil of yours for many years." Though his English was perfect, his measured voice was tinged with the suggestion of a French accent.

Dorian snorted from where he stood at Titus's left shoulder, also deceptively calm as a panther about to spring. "I'd give you terrible marks. Look at you, you're here alone with no army at your back. You're obviously going to die."

"I'd rather no one die today," Morley said, belying the rifle he'd tucked into his shoulder.

Dorian expressed a sigh of consternation, adjusting his eye patch. "You've always been *such* a boor, Morley. I can't fathom how we've become allies."

The chief inspector ignored him. "Where are the security officers hired to protect these women?"

"He told them to go home!" Mercy gestured to the gangster, her features a mask of ardent disbelief. "We brought *five* useless armed brutes with us, but he somehow arrived here first. When he introduced himself and told our guards to go…well they just… *left.*"

"They'd doubtless heard of me." Raphael Sauvageau's laughing, tawny eyes locked with Titus, and something like recognition flared there. "*You* are the dangerous one, Doctor," he murmured as if to himself. "One of these women belongs to you." He circled the girls, making a great show of inspecting them, not as a man, but as a beast might his next meal. "The question is, which? The bespectacled bluestocking, the mouthy minx, or..." He stopped in front of Nora, whose features remained carefully blank, her composure born of years of living with volatility. "Ah yes, the benighted beauty."

"If you touch her—" Titus lunged forward, but Dorian caught his shoulder.

"I haven't, and I don't intend to." Sauvageau put up his hands in a gesture of mock surrender as Morley drew a bead. "There's no need for all of that. It is only my brother, Gabriel, and me. We mean no one harm."

Another man stepped from behind the stacked crates to take up sentinel behind the women. He wore a long coat over shoulders half again as wide as his brother's, and a curious hood that shielded his features from view. He said nothing. He didn't need to. The way he loomed over the women spoke terrifying volumes.

Raphael kept his tone conversational, genial even. "We only needed the two of us to load our gold into the cart and we will be on our way."

"Horseshit," Dorian spat. "Surely your savages are close by."

"*Fauves*, not savages." Raphael's eyes gleamed with a dangerous ire. "We are untamed but elegant beasts. We aren't like the brutes and bullies here. We are teaching men to find their own sovereignty. To create their own class in a system that would repress them."

Morley made a distinctly British sound of disgust before he muttered, "Bloody French, even their gangsters are *vogue*."

"Monegasque," Raphael corrected. "Half English, actually, but that isn't what you need to worry about... *your* current problem, is that I stand between you and your women, and you stand between me and the door through which I need to carry my gold. Fortunately for all of us, these challenges are easily resolved."

Morley cocked his rifle. "You've balls of brass. I'll give you that. But you're insane if you think you're walking out of here with that gold."

"Say I don't." An edge leaked into the gangster's voice, turning his consonants lethally sharp. "Like you, Dorian Blackwell, I have a long memory. I do not forget what is taken from me, and I always take what I'm owed…would it do for any of you to wallow in wonder over when I'll chose to collect on the debt? Because there *will* be a reckoning. I am just as relentless as any of you. Dare I say more so." He plucked at a loose fiber from Nora's sleeve, and only the delicate flare of her nostrils advertised her panic. "No one in this room would be safe."

This time no one stopped Titus when he advanced. "I will end you, Sauvageau."

The pile of muscle behind the girls unsheathed a knife. He did nothing with it, but each woman tensed at the sound, the twins reaching for their elder sister.

On anyone else, Sauvageau's smile would have been disarming. "Correct me if I'm wrong, Doctor, but did you not take an oath to do no harm?"

Titus wasn't a doctor right now. He was a man. A man come to claim his woman, to snatch her out of the jaws of a monster.

And then throttle her with his bare hands.

"I'm a surgeon," he hissed. "Which means I know *exactly* how to carve into you until your voice would give out from the screaming."

Raphael glanced back at Nora with an impressed expression. "I do believe he loves you."

She stared at him, her heart shining in her eyes. "I love him."

Titus almost dropped the implements in his hands. To hear the words from her mouth for the first time stole his breath. But the fear that they could be her last words filled him with a dread he'd not known possible.

"And so we find ourselves at an impasse." The gangster clapped his hands together. "Kill me and take my gold, and start a gang war the likes of which this city has not seen. Let me go and take my gold, then look over your shoulders until I come for it... and for you. Leave now and give me back my gold. And be done with the entire business." He opened his arms like a benevolent king before turning to Nora. "The Fauves have no dealings with you or yours, and the Chief Inspector saved me from having to kill your husband for stealing from me in the first place." He glanced at Titus. "Did you a favor, I think."

"But—but what about the clinics?" Felicity's panicked question echoed through the room like the ricochet of a bullet. When the gangster turned to her, Felicity gasped, putting her hand to her mouth as she visibly began to shake. Behind her lenses, her clear, blue eyes went owlish and round as wells of tears gathered in spikes in her lashes.

"What's this you say?" Raphael glided toward her with a serpentine grace, and she took several steps backward, tripping on the hem of her gown.

Gabriel caught her shoulders with lightning reflexes. The wicked knife still in his hands, the flat of the blade resting against her arm.

She looked at it and whimpered, going slack like a frightened bunny in the enormous man's grip. Her skin blanched a ghostly shade and her breath started to sob into her throat as if she couldn't gulp enough air.

Raphael held out a hand, but paused when she shrank away. "*You* needn't fear me, child. What do you mean about the clinics?"

"I—I can't...I—I..." Felicity broke off, beginning to hyperventilate in earnest.

"Back away, sir." Mercy lunged forward and slapped Raphael's hand aside. "She cannot breathe when she is frightened!" She yanked her sister toward her and, to Titus's astonishment, the silent and mysteriously hooded Gabriel released Felicity from his grip and retreated toward the water, sheathing the knife immediately.

Something about his posture told Titus that he was not...unaffected by the encounter.

Strange.

For his part, Raphael gazed down at the hand that'd been slapped away as if truly seeing it for the first time, and then up at Mercy with an arrested expression.

As if sensing danger, Nora stepped forward, thrusting herself between Sauvageau and her younger sisters. "You asked when we arrived, why we'd chosen now to come for the gold you'd lost."

"Not lost," Raphael corrected. "It was taken."

She flicked a glance at Titus, looked away, and then back as if she couldn't help herself. She stared at him, though she answered the gangster. "The reason we thought to...recover the gold was to give it to Dr. Conleith, so he could properly operate and finance the surgeries he's building in the city."

Titus was only paces from her now, but he couldn't reach her, not without the risk of Sauvageau doing something dangerous. "Nora... what the devil?"

Sauvageau rested his elbow on his folded forearm, crooking his finger against his chin. "I've seen these surgeries in the city. I thought they were called Alcott's."

"Doctor Preston Alcott was a mentor of mine," Titus explained, hoping to take the focus from Nora. "One who has passed."

Sauvageau nodded. "Conleith is a bit too Irish for current times, I suppose." He looked Titus up and down. "You're young for such a celebrated surgeon."

"No older than you, I'd wager."

"Touché." A dark brow lifted. "I assume you didn't send your ravishing lover and her entourage to procure you this gold."

"I'd never," Titus vowed before sending Nora a hard look. "She'd insisted she didn't know where it was."

"She only learned of this warehouse last night," Mercy rushed to explain, whilst still rubbing a hand over Felicity's back as she glared imperiously at Sauvageau. "This was *supposed* to be her grand gesture, and *you* are ruining it."

Raphael's dark eyes lit with amusement even as he said, "I've ruined a great many things, and people, Miss Goode, but this is the first time a grand gesture has fallen victim to my name."

Titus was as irate as he was confused. "Grand gesture? Nora, what is she on about?"

Nora rubbed at her eyes as though to wipe away tears, but they remained curiously dry.

Mercy fielded the question before she could summon an explanation. "We—Felicity and I—told Nora that we didn't give a fig about husbands, or our reputations, and so she doesn't have to marry the Duke's son. We thought that if we could retrieve the money you needed for your clinics, then you might forgive her for leaving you...even if it *was* partly to save you." She tossed her golden curls. "Again."

"*Mercy*," Nora hissed.

Everyone in the room fell away until, in Titus's vision, there was only her, dressed in raven black, her pale skin gilded by lamplight. "Is this true?"

She glanced around at their audience and drew a steadying breath as she drifted to the edge of the platform. "I thought..." She hesitated. Swallowed. Once.

179

Twice. "I *knew* that if you loved me, you stood to lose everything, and I couldn't live with that. But I imagined that if... if I could give you the fortune you stood to lose, we could possibly see a way to—to be together."

His anger welled to the surface. "You could see a way. *You* could see a way, Nora, because the path has always been clear to me. I told you that."

She shook her head, her eyes fathomless wells of regret. "I realize you think that now. But I've seen what the loss of fortune does to a man. It drove my husband to the very depths of madness. To do unspeakable things and to ally himself with criminal dregs."

"You wound me, my lady." Sauvageau covered his heart as if she'd pierced it. "After I've worked so hard to fashion myself as the criminal elite."

She went on as if he wasn't even there. "William hated me in the end... did you know that? That a man can love and hate at the same time? It is an ugly thing, Titus. I couldn't have born that from you. It would have destroyed me to watch the light leave your eyes. To see those who respect you turn their backs. To watch as doors are slammed in your face and friends desert you. You might think that you're strong enough to survive that, and maybe you are... but I'm not. This city needs you. The world needs what you're going to discover. The miracles you'll perform."

Titus suddenly wished he could sit down. It all made a bit more sense now. This entire time he'd expected her to trust him. To understand what he wanted and what he meant for them and to believe that he could bring it all to pass. However, in doing so, he'd forgotten that the men in Nora's life were forever making decisions for her. And she'd been tossed about on that turbulent sea like a boat with torn sails and no anchor.

What cause had she to believe in anyone?

"Nora, I—"

A heartrending sob broke through the noise, and they all turned to see Felicity bravely holding both hands over her mouth, now, as hot tears streamed from her eyes.

Raphael, who seemed to have made a point to remain close by, handed Felicity a handkerchief as the soft-hearted girl wept.

She stared at it for a moment, as if it might bite her, then reached out and took it.

The gangster's face softened in miraculous increments. "You must be possessed of a heart as cold as mine, Miss Goode, to remain unmoved by their plight."

She sniffled and dabbed at her eyes, her lashes wiping at the fog of her spectacles. "I just... I thought I'd arranged a happy ending..."

His mercurial noise might have been a chuckle. "You are a clever girl. You don't really believe there is such a thing as a happy ending, do you?"

"Of course I do." She emitted a hiccupping sigh before taking several hitching breaths. "I believe that sometimes the stars can align. That one change of heart can change the course of fate. That forgiveness and love are possible, even against the most terrible odds...even for someone like you."

Raphael snorted and started to retort. Then, as if he heard a summons no one else did, he turned to the shadowy corner of the room where the hooded figure stood. "Permit me to confer with my brother a moment." He strode to Gabriel, where they held court in rapid, quiet French.

After several bombastic and crude gestures, he returned, wearing a carefully blank look. It was impossible to tell if he'd won or lost.

"Gabriel and I have come to a conclusion," he announced from between clenched teeth. "It seems we wish to make a charitable donation, enough to build a handful of hospitals."

"Oh come off it," Dorian Blackwell called from the dark. "*No one* is *that* altruistic."

"I do not disagree. Consider it a payment, Doctor Titus Conleith, for a surgery you will perform in the future. Buy the best instruments. Attend the most important lectures and instructional theaters on the reconstruction of bones and skin. And pray that your skills are what they are reputed to be when next we darken your doorstep."

Before Titus could ask more, the man clicked his boots and bowed. "We'll be in touch." Curiously, he paused to pluck his handkerchief from Felicity's lax fingers, and smirked over at Mercy's dumbstruck expression. "Surely *that* fulfills the requisites for a grand gesture."

She merely gawked at him, slack-jawed, and uncharacteristically speechless.

Instead of waiting for an answer, he turned to the silent figure in the corner, and they strode into the darkness.

After a pregnant moment, Dorian gathered himself and strode toward the door. "I'm going after them."

"Don't." Morley held him back.

"But, Titus can't serve as surgeon to *two* gangsters. It just isn't done."

Morley eyed him with a hound-like petulance. "I thought you were legitimate."

"I am... mostly." Dorian sucked his teeth. "Even so, that upstart bastard irks me."

"Only because he reminds you of yourself not so long ago before you *supposedly* reformed."

Titus could do nothing but stare at Nora as their banter faded into the background.

She loved him. She'd just said so. She did all this... for him.

For his forgiveness. For a chance.

A latent growl worked its way from deep in his chest and burst forth as he dropped his weapon and bag, lunged for her, and swept her into his arms.

"*Titus*," she gasped, flailing for a moment before locking her arms around his neck to secure herself as he marched toward Blackwell's carriage. "What the devil are you doing?"

"Something I should have done ages ago," he gritted out.

Felicity rushed after them, but Morley seized her elbow and redirected her. "We'll take another coach," he said, exchanging a knowing look with Blackwell.

Titus nodded at the driver, who jumped down and opened the door so he could unceremoniously plunk Nora down on the luxurious seat and follow her inside.

THE LONG ROAD

*N*ora did her best to head off a lecture. "You don't have to condescend to me about the foolishness of this endeavor, but I couldn't have known our hired security would go running at the first sight of trouble," she began as Titus tucked his long legs into the coach and shut them in together, creating a tight oasis of luxurious cobalt.

"Are you hurt?" he asked in a carefully bland and measured voice.

The question warmed her. "I'm all right. They never touched me."

"Good." Instead of uncoiling at her answer, his jaw locked together as if to keep from roaring. "Now what in *God's* name do you think you were trying to—"

She put up a staying hand. "I know you're angry—"

"You can't *begin* to imagine what I'm feeling right now." He broke off, a muscle working furiously just below his temple as he simply stared at her, his eyes glinting with an emotion she was truly incapable of defining.

Nevertheless, Nora absorbed his features with all the appreciation of a prisoner glimpsing the light of day for the first time in years. His golden eyes were haunted by shades, and deeper grooves sprouted from their edges. Ashen skin stretched more tightly over his dramatic cheekbones, and a few days' growth of beard widened his jaw from masculine to dangerous. His clothes were rumpled and he smelled of whiskey.

He looked truly awful.

He was the most beautiful man alive.

And he'd come for her. It was all she could do not to grin in the face of his temper. To beam with a light she was afraid could not last.

"What did they mean?" he rumbled in a voice edged with lethal calm. "Mercy said you saved me... again."

Nora allowed guilt to pull her gaze down to where their knees almost touched. "Mercy says a lot of things."

"And your father, he said he deserved my anger...why?"

A little tremor coursed through her. She'd promised herself to never burden him with this truth, but perhaps she'd been mistaken. "I think... you know why."

"I want to hear it from you."

Nora collapsed back on the seat, letting her head fall against the damask velvet as she affixed her stare somewhere above his unruly hair. "I married William all those years ago because...Papa threatened you if I didn't."

His fists curled on his thighs, and his every muscle bunched, but Nora forced herself to continue.

"He vowed that he'd make certain no school would accept you and no household would employ you. That he might have you thrown in prison or worse. He went so far as to threaten to put me in an institution, as well. It all seemed so hopeless, and you had such dreams, such ambition and promise. I—I loved you too much to condemn you to that. I didn't think sacrificing a girl you'd only been attached to for three months would be so bad as losing everything you ever—"

"Three months," he echoed, the syllables drawn out

carefully as he leaned forward. "Three months? *You* only loved *me* for three months. I loved you since the moment I laid eyes on you."

That snapped her gaze back to his solemn features. "Impossible. You were ten when we met."

"And you were the dream I didn't dare to allow myself to hope for, even then."

Defeat followed quickly on the elation he'd evoked with those words. Nora dropped her head in her hands and hid, so she didn't have to look at the mess she'd made of everything. "And now...I'm a nightmare."

His knees hit the floor of the carriage, and he reached for her wrists. Pulling her hands away from her eyes, he slid his fingers over her jaw until he held her face cupped in his palms. He looked down at her as if she were a revelation, his gaze suddenly tender, though his features remained taut with an agonizing emotion. "My entire life I've been certain that I loved you considerably more than you would ever love me, and I'd made my peace with that. But... God, Nora, if I'd only known—"

Those two words. *If only*. They'd driven her mad before.

She shook her head, new tears sliding down her burning cheeks and landing in his palms. "I *died* the day you left. I've done so many things in my life I regret, but hurting you that night has always been my most egregious sin. I never even cared if my subsequent actions doomed me to hell, because hell is living in a world where you were close and yet impossible to reach. And now I fear that even with all I've been through, nothing's changed. I am still ruined."

"Not to me." His grip tightened, his thumb silencing her as he traced the outline of her lips. "Listen, Nora. I am merely a doctor, but as you see, I have powerful friends. Your father couldn't *wish* to have a circle of influence like mine. The Chief Inspector. Dorian Blackwell and his wife, the Countess Northwalk. The Duke and Duchess of Trenwyth. The Earl and Countess of Southbourne... I could go on—"

"Don't you understand," she interrupted. "These are the people I could drive away with the scandal attached to my name."

To her utter astonishment, a rumble of mirth vibrated from him. "You don't know these people, but you will. And they'll support you. They'll dare the rest of the *ton* to shame you. And even if they did, Nora, we'd keep other society. This is a whole wide city full of people. Hang everyone but you and me."

For some humiliating reason, this only made her weep harder.

He thumbed away her tears, only to have them replaced with new ones. "You said something to me that has been weighing on my conscience..."

"What's that?" she sniffed, trying to regain control of herself.

"That you don't know who you are. That you don't feel that you are deserving, but *I* know you, Nora. Every man in your life has made you feel unworthy but, darling, you are kind and self-sacrificing. You've always made yourself responsible for others in your care. Your family, your bastard of a husband, your sisters. I could lift that burden from you. I could care for you, so that you might turn your kindness elsewhere. You can find whatever purpose suits you. And I'll be right beside you, if you'll let me."

Overwhelmed, Nora gripped his arms, intent upon pulling him away, but she couldn't bring herself to do it. Not when he was right in front of her, kneeling between her knees, saying the words that filled the empty well of her soul. "I...don't—I can't believe this is happening."

"Why not?"

"Because every time I've dared myself to hope, it's

been ripped from me... and I allowed it. I facilitated it. When I think of the time we've lost, of all the things I could have said and done differently..." She laid her palms on his chest, searching for the thrum of his heart and finding it there, strong and steady. "I realize it was irresponsible to come for the gold, but I wanted to do *something* to fix what I'd broken. I was desperate and reckless..."

He broke her words off with a searing kiss, his lips a warm and reassuring pressure against hers, parting her lips so she could taste the salt of her tears. He kept the kiss gentle and voluptuous, his tongue slick and soft against hers, making no demands. Asking nothing. Just offering. Coaxing.

He pulled back before the kiss could deepen any further, though the pace of his heart had quickened beneath her palm.

"God, I love you," he breathed against her mouth, the hands bracketing her face roaming to cup her head and smooth down her neck. "I didn't need a grand gesture or a crate of gold any more than you need ask my forgiveness. I'm not angry, I should never have been angry. Medicine is my calling, but *you* are my life. Nora." He kissed her temples, "Nora..." her eyelids and brow, "my lovely Nora." He smoothed his lips over her cheek until he returned to her mouth. "You are the greatest treasure. The sparkle beneath a grey sky. You are the beauty no one else can compare to."

"How blind you are," she said wryly, expecting any moment to wake from a dream.

He pulled back to spear her with a look full of so much affection, she nearly expired from the dizzy optimism it evoked. "I can only see you. Here. Right in front of me. We decide our futures now. You and I. Nora, will you marry me?"

She gripped his shoulders, suddenly frantic. "Yes. To-day. *Right* now. Before anything happens to stop it."

He chuckled, fondly caressing her hair. "Nothing will happen. Nothing will take you from my arms. Never again. Not if you come to me with your worries and burdens. Not if you let me in to help you. I want to protect you. I want that to be my right and privilege. The whole world could collapse tomorrow and all I'd want is to experience it with you. Would you promise to let me?"

Ardent emotion robbed her of her words, so she simply nodded, her fingers curling in his lapels to draw him down for another luxurious, whisky-flavored kiss. One that deepened and heated as his fingers ventured possessively over her skin.

Nora sighed into his mouth, releasing with the breath a tremulous marvel at the machinations of the day. She'd been heartsick only last night. And now her love was in her arms.

She couldn't bear to think of the dismal years and treacherous road they'd had to take to find each other.

But as his fingers began to caress their way up the silk of her stockings, she was very glad, indeed, of the long road back home.

EPILOGUE

SIX MONTHS LATER

$\mathcal{T}$itus applauded with the exuberance of the crowd as his beaming wife handed a pair of scissors to the Duchess of Trenwyth. Once the ribbon was cut and a picture taken for the press, the citizens of Southwark were treated to refreshments and libations, even a few happening by on their way from work.

Though the venture was his, Titus was more than content to step away from the hubbub around the attractive and wildly popular duke and duchess. He allowed the press of people to crowd him out, until he found himself leaning against a stoop across the street, hovering by an alley.

This was a year of dreams realized, and he selfishly wanted a moment to savor it.

Many souls gathered to see that Alcott's Southwark Surgery had expanded to a proper clinic with gleaming instruments and a brand-new surgical theater with a staff of three noted physicians and six capable nurses.

Similar surgeries in Whitechapel, South Bank, Lambeth, Greenwich, and Hampstead were under construction. In thanks not only to an influx of, admittedly, ill-gotten gold, but also the patronage of several philanthropists and Titus's own profits from Knightsbridge.

And in the center of it all, was Nora.

At first, of course, their marriage had been met with a chaos of scandal, most of which they avoided with a honeymoon in Italy, France, and a lovely yachting trip to Greece.

Upon their return, the Duchess of Trenwyth and her influential Ladies' Aid Society clutched Nora to their collective bosoms and began a full-scale society campaign the likes of which even the Prime Minister would be proud.

He and Nora had taken up riding again in Italy, and had purchased several mounts to keep in the city. They'd escape the office for a bracing gallop, and he'd watch her hair fly out behind her, her lips parted in the smile that graced her mouth more readily these days. Her sister Prudence promised to join her just as soon as she could climb on a horse after her and Morley's child arrived.

With the Duchess of Trenwyth at Nora's side when he could not be, trotting through the park was again a friendly venture. She'd become more of a celebrity than a pariah, and her narrative had all the salacious notes of Lady Godiva, a rebel rather than a ruined woman.

There were naysayers and gossips, of course. And her father and mother had all but publicly disowned her, but Nora met the pain of it with her head held high and her heart open. On top of her philanthropic endeavors, she worked by his side, providing comfort to the sick and protection to women, coordinating escapes in some cases and empathetic advice in others.

She was happy with their life—with him—or so she kept insisting as they lay entwined each night, slick and exhausted and no less ecstatic for it.

And he was glad, even though happiness didn't even come close to describing what he felt.

He was...complete.

Life wasn't perfect; in fact, chaos and calamity commanded most of his days. Suffering and death were part of a surgeon's existence. But no matter the misery he was subjected to, she was the soothing caress that had become the balm to his soul.

They laughed together. Teased and tormented each other. Spent lively meals with friends and made plans to travel and take holidays.

It was a life many men could only dream of... and here he was living it.

A smile tugged at the corner of his lips and a wash of awareness warmed his skin, alerting him that she was nearby before she melted from the crowd.

A vision in a frothy scarlet gown with a matching black hat, she drew the eye of every man in her vicinity as she glided toward him with a radiant smile.

"It's a bracing burden to have such a lovely wife, but I suppose it is a cross I must bear," he purred as she melted into his side and tipped her head to rest her temple against his shoulder.

"Why do you think I came searching for you?" She beamed up at him, black cherry eyes twinkling with mirth. "The ladies of Southwark were beginning to gather in this direction, I had to come and stake my claim. They'll be fabricating all sorts of ills to have you examine them."

"You're patently ridiculous." He dropped an adoring kiss into her hair. "We should leave," he whispered. "I'm already bored of this."

She laughed, knowing they both would stay for the duration, and collapse in a depleted heap at the end of the day. It was a game of theirs, to plan their social escapes. One they'd started to play when the anxiety of a gathering would overwhelm her in the early days of her return to society.

She scanned the crowd milling about. "All we'd have

to do is melt into this alley. Where should we go, husband? Should we ride in the park?"

"I'd love a ride," he growled against her ear. "But we might get arrested for indecency if we do it in the park."

She swatted his chest, then froze.

"What is it?" he asked, instantly on alert.

Instead of answering, she tugged on his sleeve, gesturing with her gaze, across the way to the fringes of the gathering.

A hooded figure stood staring right at them, his preternatural stillness seeming to make him invisible to those who teemed around him.

Gabriel Sauvageau.

Titus stared back, not in challenge but in acceptance. He dipped his chin in greeting.

Gabriel did the same before melting into the crowd and disappearing into an alley.

"What do you think he wanted?" she asked. "We've not seen or heard from the Fauves since Sheerness. But I worry about them sometimes... about what they'll ask you to do."

Titus shook his head, still staring at the corner around which the man had disappeared. "They didn't have to leave the gold. I don't care who needs medical attention, I would give it to them. It's my responsibility to treat a wound. Doesn't matter what sort of person they are, that's for better men than I to judge."

"There *is* no better man than you," Nora said, rising on her toes to press a soft kiss to his cheek so she could whisper in his ear. "You stitched my life back together when I thought no one could...and *that*, dear husband, is why I will always love you."

ALSO BY KERRIGAN BYRNE

A GOODE GIRLS ROMANCE
Seducing a Stranger
Courting Trouble
Dancing With Danger
Flirting With Disaster

THE BUSINESS OF BLOOD SERIES
The Business of Blood
A Treacherous Trade
A Vocation of Violence

VICTORIAN REBELS
The Highwayman
The Hunter
The Highlander
The Duke
The Scot Beds His Wife
The Duke With the Dragon Tattoo
The Earl of Christmas Past

THE MACLAUCHLAN BERSERKERS
Highland Secret
Highland Shadow
Highland Stranger
To Seduce a Highlander

THE MACKAY BANSHEES

Highland Darkness
Highland Devil
Highland Destiny
To Desire a Highlander

THE DE MORAY DRUIDS
Highland Warlord
Highland Witch
Highland Warrior
To Wed a Highlander

CONTEMPORARY SUSPENSE
A Righteous Kill

ALSO BY KERRIGAN
The Highwayman
The Hunter
The Highlander
The Duke
The Scot Beds His Wife
The Duke With the Dragon Tattoo
How to Love a Duke in Ten Days
All Scot And Bothered

ABOUT THE AUTHOR

Kerrigan Byrne is the USA Today Bestselling and award winning author of THE DUKE WITH THE DRAGON TAT-TOO. She has authored a dozen novels in both the romance and mystery genre. Her newest mystery release THE BUSINESS OF BLOOD is available October 24th, 2019

She lives on the Olympic Peninsula in Washington with her dream boat husband. When she's not writing and researching, you'll find her on the water sailing and kayaking, or on land eating, drinking, shopping, and taking the dogs to play on the beach.

Kerrigan loves to hear from her readers! To contact her or learn more about her books, please visit her site: www.kerriganbyrne.com

CPSIA information can be obtained
at www.ICGtesting.com
Printed in the USA
BVHW081809011220
594459BV00007B/135